SUCCUBUS BARGAIN

THE (UN)LUCKY SUCCUBUS

SUCCUBUS HAREM SERIALS 1-5

L.L. FROST

SUCCUBUS BARGAIN

The (un)Lucky Succubus Book 1

This is a work of fiction. Names, characters, businesses, places, events and incidents are either the products of the author's imagination or used in a fictitious manner. Any resemblance to actual persons, living or dead, or actual events is purely coincidental.

Cover & Book Design by L.L. Frost

Printed in the United States of America.

First Printing, 2017

ALSO BY L. L. FROST

THE VEIL UNIVERSE

The (un)Lucky Succubus

First Serialized in Succubus Harem

Succubus Bargain

Succubus Studies

Succubus Mission

Succubus Hunted

Succubus Dreams

Succubus Trials

Succubus Undone

Succubus Reborn

Succubus Ascended

Demonic Messes (And Other Annoyances)

Drunk Girl *(novella)*

Doom Dog *(novella)*

The Cleaners

The Witchblood

The Fox God

Tally & Her Witches

MONSTERS AMONG US

Monsters Among Us: Hartford Cove

First Serialized in Hartford Cove

A Curse of Blood

Bathe Me In Red

A Feud to Bury

HelloHell Delivery

"Excuse me, ma'am." A teenage kid nods politely as he holds the door and waits for me to shuffle through into the coffee shop.

I push my sunglasses tighter against my face and pause inside for a moment while my eyes adjust to the interior lighting that casts a shadowed haze over the round, crowded tables and leather upholstered chairs.

With a shiver, I pull the voluminous sweatshirt closer, despite the mid-July heat. My skin aches, tight and itchy with a dryness no amount of moisturizer can smooth away. I've abstained from my energy feedings too long, and now my body devours itself to stay alive.

My nostrils flare in search of the telltale scent of another demon and find none. Instead, I breathe in the bitter, rich aroma of coffee, and under it, the warm, salty musk of humans. Saliva fills my mouth, my jaw aching with hunger. Every person I pass smells like a walking happy meal right now.

I search the room in case my senses are failing, but I'm the only demon in the small shop. My contact hasn't shown up yet. When I check my watch, I discover I arrived early. Giving myself a few more minutes before I left home would have allowed me to avoid being surrounded by so much temptation. But hunger got the better of me, and I'd left the apartment in such a hurry I forgot my wallet.

Luckily, the pants I grabbed still have cash in the pockets. I can buy a coffee to warm myself up while I wait.

Despite the crowd, no line forms at the counter, and I make my way farther into the store, hands stuffed into my pockets to keep them away from temptation.

"Welcome, ma'am!" The young man behind the counter smiles, bright-white teeth flashing in his tanned face. "What can I get for you, today?"

He gets bonus points for not giving my unusual attire a strange look. A giant sweatshirt stands out amid the brightly colored shorts and tank tops worn by most of the patrons. With my white hair, tipped blue at the ends, and the pallor of my skin, he probably assumes I'm a goth transplant from one of the big cities.

"Large, raspberry mocha, extra whip." I lick my dry lips as my gaze drops to the tempting pink of his narrow mouth.

His hand hovers over a stack of cups, unaware of his danger. "Iced?"

"Hot, please."

He pulls one of the large, cardboard cups from a stack and poises a sharpie over it. "Name?"

"Adie." I rip my eyes away from the pink flash of tongue and turn my attention to the food display.

"Would you like anything to eat?"

His super happy tone grates on my nerves, and I want to drag him over the counter and shut him up with my mouth.

Nails digging into my palms, I force a smile. "No, thank you."

He taps at the screen in front of him for a moment. "That will be eight fifty-three."

I frown. "You can't be serious."

The bright smile wobbles with uncertainty as he points upward. "You ordered a large mocha with an add flavor, right?"

Above his head, the menu board lists out the

prices. He's really not kidding. When did coffee become so expensive?

"Yeah, that's right." I pull out my wad of dollar bills, unfolding them one at a time as I make a mental note to jack up the cost of the espresso I plan to serve at my future bakery.

Over the buzz of conversation, the bells at the entrance jingle, followed by the quiet clip of dress shoes against tiled floor. The cashier's smile spreads into a full-on grin as he glances over my shoulder at the new customer.

The smell of ozone curls around me to tickle at my senses. A demon. My fingers spasm, and the last bill falls to the floor.

"Here, allow me." The throaty purr drags along my too sensitive skin like the finest silk sheets.

I lean my hip against the low counter and risk a peek as he crouches to retrieve the money. Dark, chestnut-brown hair forms neat waves across the top of his head. Broad shoulders stretch the limits of his black suit jacket, and designer jeans lovingly outline strong, muscular thighs.

He rises smoothly to his feet and holds out the crinkled dollar bill. Black eyes meet mine from beneath thick eyebrows, and my lips part, dragging the metallic burn of his scent across my tongue and into my belly.

If humans are happy meals, this demon is triple-chocolate decadence cake.

His eyes narrow, nostrils flaring as he takes in my own scent, and frowns. Annoyance ripples through me, squashing some of my excitement. He's not what I expected either, but he doesn't need to look so surprised. I snatch the bill from his fingers and turn back to the cashier to finish paying for my over-priced mocha.

"How long will my coffee take?" I demand, rude and not giving a damn about it. I just need to get this over with quickly.

His boss should give him a raise for the way his smile stays in place. "There's two online orders ahead of you, but it shouldn't be more than five minutes."

I ignore the change he tries to return and stuff my hands into my pockets. "Where's the bathroom?"

"Down the hall to the left." He points toward a service hall hidden behind the barista stand, where a sign announces the restrooms.

"Thanks." With a pointed glance at the demon behind me, I shuffle toward the hallway.

"What can I get for you, sir?" A new level of

warmth fills the cashier's voice as the demon takes my place.

"A small drip coffee, please."

The unisex sign on the door swings as I push it open and step inside, letting the door shut behind me.

The single occupant bathroom makes an effort at coziness. Painted warm coffee-brown, with dim lighting and a box of potpourri in a basket next to the sink, it mostly masks the lemon cleaner they used to sanitize the place recently. Quiet music, flutes and a guitar melody, filters in through speakers on the wall.

My tennis shoes squeak across the tiles, and I poke at the dried contents of the basket with distaste. Lavender and cedar. How disgusting. Like old people smell.

At least they didn't use any frankincense. That nasty stuff makes me sneeze for days.

A moment later, the door opens and closes behind me, followed by the snick of the lock.

I meet the demon's eyes in the mirror. "Julian sent you? From HelloHell Delivery?"

His eyes widen for a moment before he nods.

"You ordered a meal?" He shrugs out of his jacket and hangs it from the hook on the back of the door. "Succubi don't usually let themselves get so…"

"You're not being paid to care about my appearance." I shove away from the sink and march over to him, determined to get this over with.

Why I let my cousin talk me into a mail-order meal still bewilders me. I blame desperation brought on by my forced crash diet from human contact. I'm officially the first succubus in demon history to lack the ability to feed through dreams.

Physically going out to feed myself takes so much time and effort, which I don't have while I work to get my bakery up and running.

I grab the demon's arm and tug him forward. "Sit on the toilet."

"Whatever works for you." His hands go to the hem of my sweatshirt. "Let's make you more comfortable."

I slap him away. "I don't need that."

He sprawls onto the toilet seat lid, long limbs spread wide. One eyebrow lifts as he stares up at me. "Won't it be better for your wings?"

"Like a quick energy pull will get my wings out." I lift shaky hands to his shoulders, dragging in another breath. He smells so delicious. My stomach tightens with anticipation.

"Are you sure?" His fingers trail up the outside of

my leggings, leaving fire in their wake. "You seem pretty desperate."

"Should food talk this much?" My hands move to cup his neck, and my skin stings where it touches his, like sleeping limbs waking up.

"Can I interest you in an upgrade?"

Unwillingly, my eyes drop to the front of his jeans. Something like that would hold me over better than the simple draw I paid for. But I'm not desperate enough to buy sex. Even if I could afford it. Which I can't.

"What I ordered is enough."

His hands drift higher. "I'll give you a discount."

"Shut up. My coffee's going to get cold." When his mouth opens again, I seal it with my lips.

His heat burns, the energy inside him a swirl of lava waiting to fill me up. A shiver of surprise goes through me. I never would have imagined my cousin's service would have such a powerful demon on the menu.

Especially not at the price I paid.

My thumbs stroke the rough stubble of his cheeks, and he opens wider to let me lap against his tongue. Power slides down my throat to spindle in my belly, easing the ache of hunger. The chill against my bones melts beneath this new warmth, and a whimper of relief escapes, my limbs shaking as I come back to life.

An answering purr rumbles in his throat as his tongue twines around mine. Our noses bump together as I tilt my head, diving deeper within his mouth to chase more energy.

Large hands cup my hips, then slide beneath my sweatshirt to graze bare skin. The muscles along my spine ripple, an ache spreading between my shoulder blades. My wings push against my skin, ready to slide free.

My eyes spring open in shock. That shouldn't happen. I'm not a newly formed succubus, lacking all self-control. Intense black eyes stare into mine as if he can see right through my sunglasses.

Panting, I pull my mouth away. "Thank you for the meal."

"You're not done yet, are you?" He licks his lips, irises expanding to cover the whites of his eyes.

I shiver at the predatory gaze. Something doesn't feel right. I need to leave. "It's enough. Thank you."

When I try to step back, he pulls me closer. "You paid for more. I can't let you go half finished."

His red lips tempt me to come back, to pull more energy, but I resist. "I'm full."

"Liar." His head moves closer to my stomach, nostrils flaring. "I can barely smell you."

I wish I could say the same, but his scent fills the small bathroom with the metallic taste of thunderstorms. It licks across my body, thick enough to drink it from the air.

His power could be in me, a tempest that will fill me with enough energy to live for a month, if not longer. Hunger floods through me, sharper for being given a taste then told there would be no more. Temptation hooks into my resolve, tearing it into little pieces.

He smirks as he senses my weakness.

"Come here, little succubus. Let me feed you." His fingers tug the strings of my hoodie, and helpless to resist the offer, my mouth returns to his.

Instead of waiting for me to take the lead, he invades my mouth. Energy comes too, stronger now as he pushes it into me with every thrust of his tongue against mine. My knees shake as the onslaught turns my bones to liquid.

Overwhelmed, I barely notice when his hands curl around the backs of my thighs, molding my body until I straddle his lap. The hard swell of his cock pushes against my core, and I whimper, ravenous for more.

His mouth leaves mine, teeth nipping at my lower lip. His hands on my hips rock me against the hard bulge. "Do you want that, little succubus?"

I do. It's been so long since a man moved between my legs. My inner muscles clench around my empty core.

"I'll give you what you need." His throaty purr rolls like thunder over my throat, his breath heat lightning against my skin.

It will be magnificent. The hard proof presses against my entrance through the scant barrier of our clothes.

His hands slide under my sweatshirt once more to stroke up my spine. My muscles ripple, the brush of feathers pushing for release. "That's it. Let your wings out. Show me how much you want it."

Reality crashes back with the swiftness of a hammer blow. My cousin's a professional. His employees would have firm instructions on my needs. We'd discussed this in advance. No up sales.

I shove the stranger away, his back thudding against the toilet's porcelain water reservoir. "You're not from HelloHell Delivery, are you?"

"Does it matter?" He arches one thick eyebrow. "I'll give you better service than some low-level, gigolo demon."

"Fucking hell." My body abuzz with energy, I scramble off his lap.

He scowls. "What's the problem with using me instead?"

"Where's your gain?" I pat my empty pockets. Shit. I don't have anything to pay him with for the energy draw. Demons don't go around giving things away for free. "What were you going to get out of this?"

I should have stuck with humans. Stupid Cousin Julian, making this sound like an easier alternative.

He stands and adjusts his jeans, the front still sporting an impressive bulge. "Isn't sex gain enough?"

"For an incubus it is." My gaze rakes over him. "But you're not one of my kind. What are you?" I sniff the air, unable to pinpoint his type. "Some kind of chaos demon?"

"Does it really matter?" He stalks forward, a predator on the hunt.

"Fuck yes, it does." I back toward the door, reaching behind myself for the lock.

He could be a collector. Is that why he wanted to see my wings? Does he want my feathers? Succubus feathers sell fast on the black market, a one hundred percent effective aphrodisiac.

"Hey, there's nothing to be scared of." He freezes,

holding his hands up, palms faced toward me. "I don't want to hurt you."

"Who said I'm scared?" I fumble the lock open, and the bolt sliding free sounds like a gunshot in the small, tiled room.

His nostrils flare again, and he takes a tiny step forward. But the energy buzzing through me makes me fast, and I fling the door open, darting through to freedom.

He storms after me, but out in the open, I'm safe. The customers in the coffee shop give me an impenetrable shield. Demon law forbids exposing our race to humankind.

I stop at the coffee bar, where my large mocha waits. Next to it sits a small drip coffee.

The barista looks up as I take my beverage. "Hey, I was just about to throw that away. It's been ready for ten minutes now."

"Thank you." I turn and find the demon right behind me, pulling his jacket back on. I shove the cup at him. "Here, payment. We're even."

He stares down at the cup, black eyes wide with disbelief. "I don't want your treat."

I grab his hand, his skin stinging against mine, and wrap his fingers around the mocha. "It's all you're getting."

"Take it back." He thrusts the cup at me.

"No." I hide my hands behind my back. "It's payment. If I take it back, I'll still owe you."

He stares at it for a moment in consideration. "I'll throw it away, then."

My lips part, hungry gaze dropping to the coffee. "But that's mocha raspberry bliss."

Gently, he sets it on the counter and steps away. "Barista, I do not want this coffee."

The human behind the counter, busy pulling shots of espresso, glances at it in confusion. "Okay, dude, no problem. I'll toss it in a second."

I stare at the large cup, indecisive. The demon leans close, warm lips brushing against my ear. "I'll see you around, little succubus."

He takes the small cup of drip coffee off the bar and strides for the exit. His fine ass, in those hip-hugging jeans, mocks me the entire way. I could have had my nails in those luscious globes. But at what cost?

As soon as he leaves, I snatch the mocha and flee.

Energy Rights

"What the fuck, Adie?" My cousin, Julian, slams into my small apartment without knocking. "You stood up my guy. Don't think you're getting a refund."

My fingers tighten around the cupcake in my hand, and I keep my eyes focused on the swirl of icing, determined to master the gradient rose in time for my presentation tomorrow at the bank.

Julian plops into the barstool across the counter from me. "Please tell me you weren't so distracted by baking that you forgot?"

"I didn't forget." Biting my lip, I carefully spin the cupcake while making rainbow arches to form the outer petals.

"Then what happened?" He leans across the counter, head tilted to get a closer look at my face.

When he takes in the rosy flush of my cheeks, his lips purse. "Shit, you should have called to cancel if you got your mojo back. Poor Philip waited at the coffee shop for over an hour."

My hand tightens on the piping bag and a glob of purple and pink frosting spurts out. Annoyed I set the cupcake down next to my other failures. "I didn't get my mojo back."

"Darling, you're glowing right now." He frowns, head tilting the other way as his blue eyes narrow. "Well, maybe not glowing. But at least you don't look like a three-day dead corpse now."

"I wasn't that bad." I reach for the second to the last cupcake on my cooling rack. I need six perfect ones to make the cupcake bouquet, which means the next two need to be perfect.

Julian shakes his head, fine white curls bouncing. "Adie, my darling, the cousins were asking when your apartment would be available for rent."

"Pack of vultures," I mutter.

"So you found a desperate human to feed on?" With one long finger, he drags the plate of ruined cupcakes closer. "Because no way you had enough whammy left to beguile anyone."

"You know I didn't."

"I don't know that." Delicately, he picks at the

green wrapper of one cake. "I have every hope you'll be cured of this unnecessary concern for human safety and start bleeding the barbarians dry like any other normal, healthy succubus."

"Bodies are hard to hide." Not that I've ever sexed anyone to death. Hand steady, I pipe on a thick center base. "And the human scientists are already close to uncovering our race."

"Pesky evolution." Julian takes a large bite of cake, eating half of it, and frosting sticks to his nose. With his mouth full, he adds, "You should have been around a hundred years ago. Those were the days."

"Before cable TV?" I shake my head. "No, thanks."

"Youth is wasted on you." Julian rolls his empty wrapper and reaches for another cake. "These are good."

"Thanks." I rotate the one in my hand, applying the last, long arch to complete the rose. "I just hope they're good enough to impress the bank."

Julian mews in distaste. "I don't know why you're bothering."

"Because I need the loan to open my bakery." Gently, I fit the cake onto its waiting stick next to the four other perfect roses.

"Can't you just seduce an old man and have him pay for it like any other respectable woman?"

"No."

He lifts his eyebrows. "Do you have gerontophobia?"

I pause in the process of building up the last rose. "What?"

"Do old, wrinkly wieners creep you out?"

"You're disgusting."

"Your desire to work for a living is disgusting." He throws his hands up. "What's the use of being a demon if you go around pretending to be human?"

"Haven't you ever just loved doing something?"

"Yes." His eyes widen, tone serious. "But witch hunting is now forbidden."

"I can't talk to you right now."

"Why talk when we can dance?" He jumps off the stool to shake his hips, tight red vinyl short-shorts creaking with every gyration. "Let's go to the club. You need a top off. You still look a little…dry."

He's not wrong. While the energy pull from earlier brought back a lot of my vitality, my skin still itches, even after a liberal coat of lotion. "Tempting, but no."

"We can go to Buck Ruckers," he wheedles. "Demon's only. Neutral ground."

“I need to rest. Tomorrow morning will be stressful enough without clubbing all night.” I set the piping bag aside to admire the last cupcake before I add it to the bouquet. I spin the vase to check it from all angles. “What do you think?”

“I think, if they decide with their stomachs, that you’ll get your loan.” Unhappiness fills his voice.

I smile with excitement. “You really think so?”

“It’s so embarrassing to be related to you.” With a roll of his shoulders, he heads back toward the front door. “Should I send Philip over? You should go in ready to whammy them if you need it.”

The offer tempts me, the way he knows it will. It would be easy to beguile the lenders into giving me the money outright. But I want to start my business off right. “No, I’m good. But, thank you.”

“Your loss. Just don’t call me crying if things don’t work out tomorrow.” He pauses at the door and turns back, considering. “Actually, do call me. I have a contact on the black market who’s on the lookout for succubus tears.”

My eyes narrow. “You’re a horrible cousin.”

He shrugs, unrepentant. “Money’s money, right?”

I wave him away. “Have fun tonight.”

“I’d say the same, but I don’t see how it’s

possible." With a last, disparaging look around my small apartment, he leaves.

I disassemble the cupcake arrangement and carefully store the small cakes in individual holders within a cardboard box to make sure they'll be safe for travel in the morning. As I slide the box into the fridge, my cellphone vibrates on the counter. I hurry to grab it, reading the contact name.

With a sigh, I press the answer button. "Yes, Julian?"

"I forgot to mention one more thing while I was up there." In the background, the sounds of traffic flood through the line, a car horn honking. It comes through my kitchen window, too, in a strange double echo. He must still be outside my building.

I walk to the corner to glance out, spotting the red glare of his shorts at the corner crosswalk, illuminated beneath a streetlight. "Yes?"

"I have a friend looking for succubus strippers. So if the cupcake thing fails—"

"Goodnight, Julian."

I hit end and toss the phone back onto the counter, where it clatters against the gray marble surface.

Despite my best efforts, Julian's words fill me with doubt. Maybe it would be a good idea to top off a little, get my powers boosted enough so I can beguile the lender if I need to. It will just be for the loan; it's not like I'll rob the bank or anything.

Usually, a decent-sized crowd hangs out at the club down the street. It's not as big as Buck Ruckers, which lowers the risk of running into family. I haven't been inside yet, having only just moved to the area to be closer to where I hope to open my bakery. The neighborhood costs more than I'd like, but the high number of businesses means more foot traffic during the day, while the clubs and bars will bring in customers at night. With the constant flow of humanity, I can skim the surface of their emotions and stop worrying about my inability to dream walk.

I peek into the fridge to double check I closed the lid on the cupcake box. My fingers hesitate on the waxed cardboard. Should I even bring them in? Banks like charts and graphs, solid numbers to back up requests, not baked goods.

Slowly shutting the door, I hurry to my bedroom and dig out my skimpiest dress. It leaves my arms, along with most of my legs and chest, bare for maximum skin to skin contact.

As I shimmy into it, I push down the guilt. I'll only use the whammy tomorrow if it's absolutely necessary.

My body throbs to the music, a deep bass that vibrates my bones, resonating with a primal urge to dance. I lift my arms over my head, head back as I let the beat lead me.

Around me, humans press close, their bodies flowing together in an age-old mating ritual that modern sensibilities have tried to wash from them. Their cells remember, though, as their legs move in rhythm to the drums, the motion of feet propelled by instinct.

Passion, lust, happiness. They hang over the dance floor in a heavy fog that settles against my skin, dew on the morning grass, the nectar of life. My body hums with the glut of it, nearly filled to capacity.

This type of feeding takes more time, hours of being surrounded by the humans, but I haven't felt this alive in months. If I hadn't starved myself, I wouldn't have needed to order a meal from HelloHell Delivery. But, by the time I realized my desperation, I'd already depleted my reserves. In order to skim energy, I need to have a well of it already inside, a magnet that draws like to like.

Thanks to the kickstart I received from the demon

this afternoon, I now have more than enough to guarantee my loan tomorrow.

Hands slide over my waist, not the first pair tonight. I lean against the hard body to enjoy the strength of hot muscle against my back. After this next song, I'll leave, but until then, why not enjoy?

The hands move higher to cup my ribs, fingers spread to brush the undersides of my breasts. A throaty rumble comes next to my ear. "I've been watching you for a while."

I smile at the pickup line. Also not the first of the night. I sway against him. "I'm not interested."

"No?" One large hand slides down to spread over my lower stomach. "You seem interested enough to me."

Annoyed, I turn my head, ready to shut him down. The mouth-watering scent of ozone fills my nose. My eyes widen in panic. What are the odds of two demons coming to the same club?

My muscles tense, ready to flee.

"None of that, now." His broad hands tuck me closer against his body. "If you run, I'll want to chase you."

Heart hammering, I peer up at the smooth underside of his chin. In the strobe of lights overhead, his hair glows red. He's not the demon from this afternoon. I drag in another breath. But he smells similar.

I swallow past the thick lump of panic. "What do you want?"

As his body moves against mine, he glances down, his vivid-blue eyes serious. "Payment for using my club to feed on."

"I—" Frantic, I search the walls for some sign that a demon owns the club. There should be markings to warn others of our race. "I didn't know."

"That's a poor excuse." His head dips, breath hot against the curve of my neck as he inhales. "You're the little succubus who moved here two months ago, aren't you?"

"I filed my transfer paperwork." I know I did. It took three days to get all the proper stamps in place. They should have alerted any other demons I would be arriving. I received a welcome packet on my move-in day, complete with a list of demon-safe businesses. My eyes narrow. "You're club's not on the neighborhood registry."

"I'm listed under the city registry, since this building crosses the territory lines." He swings us around and points at a shrouded balcony that overhangs the club's entrance. "That's my mark, there."

I squint at the dark-gray on black swirls that form a barely visible glyph. "That hardly counts."

"And yet it does." The song changes, transitioning into something with a faster pace, and the people around us jump up and down, hands out at their sides in some modern dance style that resembles a pogo-stick. "Come, let's take this discussion to somewhere more private."

I dig in my heels. "I don't—"

"—want to leave with all that energy? I agree."

He releases me long enough to transfer his grip to my arm, his fingers a loose but inescapable shackle around my arm as he moves in front of me to pull me forward. His skin against mine tingles, like low-level electricity.

My lips part on a gasp as it shivers up my arm and down into my stomach. I stumble forward a step, a moth irresistibly drawn to the bug zapper.

"Look at all this energy." His thumb sweeps circles over the sensitive bend of my inner elbow and little sparks of static crackle between us. Lightning blue eyes catch mine, and I fall into the storm. "What do you need it all for?"

"My meeting tomorrow." Mesmerized, I let him lead me away from the dance floor and into a dimly lit hall.

"What kind of meeting?" His hand slides down to circle my wrist, trailing sparks in its wake, and I shiver.

"With the bank." I lick my lips. "For my cupcakes."

He smiles in bemusement. "Cupcakes?"

I nod, unable to take my eyes from his. "I have a bouquet."

"A bouquet of cupcakes?" Confusion wrinkles his forehead. "That you're taking to the bank."

Annoyance ripples through me, a counter wave to the flow of electricity. It disrupts whatever spell the demon wove around me, and I scowl. "Yeah, a bouquet of cupcakes. You have a problem with that?"

"It's a little unusual." He reaches up to cup my face, and tingles course down my neck. "But let's talk about this stolen energy."

"Stop that." Now that I know his trick, I won't fall for it again. I duck away from his touch, and when he reaches for me again, I snap my teeth at him. "Fuck off!"

"Oh, feisty. I like that." With a grin, he presses me against the wall, one muscular thigh pushing between my knees.

I wiggle against him, my already short dress sliding higher. "What do you think you're doing?"

"That's my energy you're filled up with." He cups my jaw, tipping my face up. His eyelids drop to veil the intensity of his gaze. "I want it back."

"The fuck it's—"

His mouth covers mine, and I clamp my teeth shut. I spent the last three hours skimming this. How dare he say it's his.

Firm lips move against mine with gentle nips that send electricity down into my stomach while his thumbs stroke my chin with coaxing pressure. I narrow my eyes at him in refusal.

His mouth curves against mine in a smile as his fingers trace down the side of my throat, then skim over my collarbone. The lightning in my belly spreads lower, warmth pooling between my legs. His thigh presses closer, against my core, and I drag in a shaky breath through my nose, flooding my lungs with the metallic tang of thunderstorms.

My mouth opens on a gasp, and his tongue slides inside, rough and invasive as he laps at my energy. A tug pulls at my core as he spindles it out of me, drinking it down, and I moan. He cups the back of my head, his head tipping to take a deeper drink, and my thighs tighten around his.

I've never had power taken from me, only the reverse, and shivers of pleasure roll through my body.

His hand grabs my ass, yanking me closer, and his hard cock rubs against my hip. Twice in one day I've had a man ready in my arms, and my core aches with the need to be filled.

Liquid heat slicks my thighs, and I reach for his ass, digging my fingers into the hard muscles. My tongue thrusts against his, moving into his mouth. His eyes widen in surprise as I latch onto the energy inside him, dragging it back into my stomach.

Did he forget I'm a succubus? Like I would give in that easy.

When he tries to release me, my hands fist in his hair to hold him in place as I swallow him down.

While giving the energy felt great, taking it roars through me with the rush of a dozen orgasms. He shudders, his legs giving out, and I ride him to the ground, straddling his chest as I continue to feast. My skin heats with the flood of power, my wings shifting restlessly beneath my skin.

When I drag myself away, my head buzzes, too full to think properly. I stare at the man beneath me and lick my lips. "Thanks for the meal."

He gives a rueful smile. "It's not quite what I planned."

I reach back to cup the front of his pants, now

wet with his release. "You got more than you deserved."

His brows arch. "You stole from my club."

"Be careful." My hand tightens around his still semi-erect cock. "I'll file a claim against you for improper display of ownership."

Undeterred by my threat to his manhood, his hands slide up my thighs, pushing the dress higher. "My glyph is up to code."

"Are you willing to bet on that?"

His pupils dilate as his hands cup my bare ass. "Are you willing to move a little higher so I can taste you?"

"And give you another chance to take my energy? Fuck, no." I lean closer to him, inhaling his lightning scent. I wasn't wrong before. His energy feels like the demon's from the coffee shop, only more stormy somehow. "What kind of demon are you?"

"The kind that desperately wants to fuck you."

"Take a nice look." I stand, legs spread on either side of his broad chest. "This is the closest you're ever getting."

(UN)LUCKY

As I stride out of the club, energy crackles beneath my skin, my wings restless in their hidden place along my spine. I want to get home, to crawl into my mound of pillows and digest like an overstuffed human after Thanksgiving.

My cell phone vibrates in the holster on my thigh. The buzz sends ticklish pleasure across my hips, and I let it ring a couple times longer than necessary, unsure if I should answer. Not a lot of people have my number, and I already spoke to Julian today, which reduces the options to one of the cousins, shudder, or my mentor, double shudder.

The phone quits as it drops to voicemail, then instantly buzzes back to life. I pause to hike the right side of my dress up to reach the damn thing, and an old man stops nearby, rheumy eyes wide as he stares at the long expanse of bared leg.

I finger wave at him before striding on, lifting the phone to my ear. “Yes?”

“Hey, Boo, what you up to?” a low voice mumbles from the other end of the line. In the background, the rat-a-tat-tat of gunfire blares.

I sigh, mood plummeting. “What do you want, Landon?”

“I heard you tried out Julian’s delivery service today?” An explosion blasts in the background. “Hey, don’t fucking throw grenades, asshole!”

“What do you want, Landon?” I repeat as a headache slowly blooms in my temples.

“Can you swing by and do a little energy share? I’m kinda low right now.” Blast. Boom! “I said stop throwing fucking grenades! Half your team is down here! Shit!”

Plastic clatters, and I picture Landon’s favorite bright-blue controller landing on a coffee table covered in porn magazines and empty water bottles.

“I’m not your supplier, Landon.” I push through the door to my apartment complex and head for the elevator. “Feed yourself.”

“Is that any way to treat your mentor?” he grumbles.

“You’re the reason I can’t transition back into

Dreamland!" I stab at the elevator's call button, foot tapping with impatience.

"Hey, don't blame that on me." He grunts and springs squeak, probably from the dilapidated couch he pulled off the sidewalk back in the nineties. "I did my best. It's not my fault you were formed from the weakest spring storm in existence. You should be grateful I bothered to collect your tiny ball of energy off the church steps."

I cringe, guilt sweeping through me. Succubus form through humans' repressed desires. Enough repression combined with an electrical storm, and poof, all those emotions create a brand-new succubus. If another of our kind is nearby, they come to collect the newly formed being and nurture it, teaching it to take form in Dreamland and feed off humans. It takes years of energy buildup before a succubus can take the next step into corporeal form.

"You know I'm grateful you took me in." The elevator arrives, and I step on, punching the button for the third floor. "But why can't you go get your own energy?"

"*Hell & Heaven* came out this week, and all my usual humans haven't slept long enough to get a good dream on." Landon specializes in video game fantasies. When new games come out, his food becomes scarce.

And therein lay the problem. Landon is addicted to the games himself and once the first home console came out, his visits to me in Dreamland became sporadic, leaving me to starve while I waited for him to remember to come lead me to dreams. Occasionally, one of my many cousins popped in and took me for a feeding, but they're all selfish scatterbrains.

It left me in a rush to go corporeal. When I formed my body decades ahead of schedule, something went wrong, and I found myself unable to re-enter Dreamland on my own.

I slept on Landon's couch for a while, hoping to learn how to fix the problem. Julian eventually took pity on me and taught me to skim off humans through skin contact. He hoped to lure me to work in one of his nightclubs. Little did he know he would give me an entirely different plan.

Open a bakery and feed off the rush of pleasure humans release when they eat sweets, while also obtaining a valid income to support myself.

"So, when will you be by?" Landon pushes as the sound of gunfire starts up once more in the background.

"I can't tonight." The elevator door slides open, and I exit onto my floor. "Besides, I didn't end up meeting with Julian's employee."

"But you fed, right?" He releases a long sigh of annoyance. "I guess I can pop into your dreamscape. When are you going to bed?"

"Don't you dare." The last thing I need is for my half-assed mentor to show up and drain me dry. "Just find a human nearby."

"It's too much work to establish myself with someone new," he groans. "Stop being selfish."

"Stop being lazy!" Annoyed, I stab in the code to unlock my apartment door and stomp inside.

His tone turns crafty. "You can't really stop me. I'm stronger than you."

My fists clench. "If you show up anywhere near my dreams, I'll sic the cousins on you."

"Brat."

"Slob."

"When are you coming over to clean?" The crinkle of plastic water bottles nearly drowns out the question. "It's getting pretty bad here."

"I'll come by next week."

I need to stop picking up after him, especially since he can more than afford a housekeeper. But

Landon's issues with strangers in his house, along with the guilt over him raising me, keeps me going back every other week.

"Thanks, Boo. You're a lifesaver."

"I'm bringing over pamphlets for a new service I found."

"Sure, sure. See you next week." The line disconnects before I can say goodbye.

I head to my bedroom and kick off my high heels with a groan before I crawl on the bed, burrowing into the mound of pillows at the top. The plush squares take up half the bed, and I pull my favorite purple sequin one against my tummy, curling around it.

The energy I gathered today fills me to bursting, more than I've consumed since becoming corporeal. If I can find a way to always be this well fed, maybe I can also figure out a way to solve my Dreamland issues.

The bakery will fix everything. I just know it.

"Shit, shit, shit."

I balance the box of cupcakes in one hand, glass

vase stuffed under my arm as I clutch my car keys in my free hand.

It took my fifth alarm clock, plugged into the outlet in my bathroom and well out of easy shut off range, to pull me from my energy-digesting coma. I now have half an hour to get across town for my meeting with the bank.

The briefcase protecting my proposal knocks against my side as I rush out of the apartment and onto the street. A tiny, white truck with flashing yellow lights on top sits next to my old sedan. When I spot the yellow boot attached to my front tire, full panic sets in.

"Excuse me!" I yell as I run toward the meter maid.

Instead of waiting, the woman walks faster as she rounds the hood of my car and practically runs for her vehicle.

"Excuse me!" I yell again, chasing after her. "I paid my parking tickets!"

"Sorry, ma'am." The woman hops up into her seat and slams the door shut, locking herself inside. Through the open window, she frowns at me. "You'll have to take that up with the city."

"But I need my car!" I grab onto the doorframe

before she can drive off. "Please, I have a meeting I need to get to."

"Not my problem." She peers down at my hand. "Remove your hand from my vehicle."

Shit. I can't afford this right now. My stomach tightens as I spindle out a thick line of energy. Doing this outside of Dreamland takes so much more out of me, and I really needed to save this for the bank. But if I miss my meeting, it won't matter how much I keep in reserves.

I shake my head until the sunglasses slide down my nose so I can look at her over the rim. "Surely we can come to an arrangement?"

"Ma'am, I must insist you remove your han—" as her sharp gaze cuts up to meet mine, her face slackens, eyes glazing over. In the next instant, she straightens, adjusting the collar of her blue, button-down shirt. "Sir, I didn't see you there. How may I help you?"

I grimace as the line of energy needed to whammy her increases. Too bad she doesn't like women, it would cost a lot less.

I step away from her small truck. "Can you please remove the boot from this car? I would really appreciate it."

"Yes, of course." The door slides open, and she hops out. Her hand moves to the top button of her shirt, popping it free to expose the shadowed valley of her breasts. "Looks like it's going to be a hot one today, don't you think?"

"Most definitely." I give her an appreciative smile as I adjust my grip on the box of cupcakes. The thin cardboard sags on one side, and I hurry to put it on the roof of my car before it folds in half.

Her soft body presses into my back. "How about we get a drink to cool off?"

A flood of images wash through my mind of the meter maid dressed in leather, one thigh high boot pressed into a man's back as she holds a whip. Her lips, a bright-crimson slash in her face, pull back from her teeth with satisfaction.

Great. A dominatrix. Which means my whammy must have transformed me into someone in need of subjugation.

I twist around and bite my lip, eyes down. "Do you think it's okay? It's so early in the day. We'd have to be fast."

"Hmm." She strokes my arm. "That doesn't sound fun, does it? How about you come over to my place after work instead?"

A picture of her personal dungeon pops up,

leather bench, concrete floors, and toys displayed on the wall. Silver rings dangle from the ceiling. I resist the urge to shudder. I don't like being tied up.

Instead, good succubus that I am, I force an interested smile. "Sounds fun."

"Please follow me. Mr. König will see you now."

"Thank you." Nervous, I twirl one of the cupcake roses to hide a dent in the frosting, then stand to follow the receptionist.

I arrived at the bank with five minutes to spare, no thanks to the persistent meter maid who insisted on writing her address on my forearm with a black sharpie. She even signed it, like we made some kind of contract of ownership right there. I adjust the sleeve of my blouse to make sure the mark stays hidden.

The receptionist leads me past a series of offices with frosted glass-paned doors, down another short hallway, and stops in front of a set of double doors made from rich mahogany. I stare at them, my fingers tightening around the glass vase as butterflies fill my stomach.

This doesn't feel right. I'm here to apply for a

small business loan. I belong in one of those offices near the front. Not deep within the bank at what appears to be the president's office.

"Are you sure I'm in the right place?" I glance around nervously. "I'm Adeline Pond."

The receptionist lifts a thick eyebrow. "Yes, Ms. Pond. Your meeting is with Mr. König."

My eyes skip to the gold plaque discreetly placed to the right of the door. It reads: *Emil König*, CEO. As in the *K* of K&B Financial.

I hastily pull off my sunglasses and stuff them into the side pocket of my briefcase as the receptionist raps his knuckles against the right hand door. It sounds deadened, as if the thick door contains a hidden layer of sound dampening material. After a heartbeat, the door swings open.

The man moves aside and extends an arm toward the office. "Please, step inside."

I smooth a sweaty palm over my pencil skirt before I walk through the door. As the receptionist leaves, closing the door behind himself, I glance around the large office. On one side of the room, a leather sofa sits in front of a fireplace, the coals cold within the hearth. Matching chairs rest on either side, with a metal coffee table in the center.

On the other side of the office, bookshelves line

the wall and a large desk dominates the space. Two chairs, small in comparison, sit in front of it. I hurry toward the desk, then pause, uncertain. Do I put the bouquet directly on it? Is that too presumptuous? I nibble my lip, eyes moving from the dark, pristine surface to my purple cupcakes.

I turn and search for a side table, something smaller and less intimidating, but find only the chairs. If I hold the vase, though, that leaves my hands tied. Maybe I should put them on the coffee table for now? The large office makes moving between the two spaces awkward. How will I easily get them for the presentation?

Around me, the air turns cold with a crisp, fresh scent, clean and silent like it gets before the first snowfall of winter. Metallic ozone underlays it, and I freeze.

"Ms. Pond, a pleasure to meet you." Even his voice sounds cold, like the rumble that precedes an avalanche.

Slowly, I turn to meet the demon's bright-blue eyes. Snow white hair slicks back from a high forehead. His pale gray suit drapes in expensive folds across broad shoulders and narrow hips.

Did I step on a luck sprite sometime in the past two days? Where did all this misfortune come from?

I straighten my shoulders with determination. "Mr. König, thank you for meeting with me."

"Please, call me Emil." His gaze drops to the vase in my hand and the corner of his mouth twitches. "Would you like to set that on the desk and take a seat?"

"Yes, thank you." I gently place the bouquet off to one side, turned so the best roses face him, and perch on the edge of the chair on the right.

He sits in the large, executive seat and leans back, comfortable. "You are here today to apply for a business loan?"

"Yes, for the start-up costs of an over-the-counter bakery."

He folds his hands on the desk. "Do you have an executive summary review?"

"Yes, right here." I open my briefcase, pull out the piece of paper, and lean forward to place it on the desk, which stands half a foot out of reach. Blood creeps up my neck as I stand to place the summary on the desk in front of him before resuming my seat.

He reads through it quickly and arches one translucent eyebrow. "You're asking for fifty-thousand dollars?"

"Yes, for rental space, reconstruction, and

equipment." My summary itemizes each of the necessary pieces to start-up the business.

He moves the piece of paper off to the side. "How much have you already invested?"

"I have the money ready to register the business, and I've created the website."

"How much revenue have you made up to this point from," his eyes cut to the bouquet, "selling cupcakes."

"None so far." I try not to flinch and open my briefcase once more, pulling out my projection charts. "But this diagram here shows how previous businesses have performed in the area."

I stand to hand him the folder, and he sets it aside without looking through it. "If other businesses have done well, then why aren't they still active?"

"The nearest one had a kitchen fire—"

"The current market leans toward health food," he interrupts. "How do you plan to entice customers to load up on sugar?"

"I'll have healthier options, as well as a full range of allergen alternatives." I dig out my sample menu, stand, and set it on the desk, refusing to sit back down as I add, "I'll also offer espresso."

He skims the list. "You expect people to pay eight dollars for coffee?"

Annoyed at his tone, the flush creeps up my neck and into my cheeks. "It's espresso and cheaper than the nearest competition."

With one finger, he pulls my executive summary back in front of himself. "I don't see a place for employee salaries. Do you have training to make good coffee?"

"I know how to make espresso." I practiced on a store-bought machine at home for hours to figure out the right dosing, grinding, and tamping to pull a perfect twenty second shot.

His gaze once more shifts to the cupcakes. "Did you bring a sample of that, as well?"

Teeth gritted, I smile. "I can bring a sample by later today, if you like."

He leans back, steepling his fingers. "I really don't see how you need fifty-thousand for this little venture."

"As you can see on the summary—"

He holds up a hand to stop me. "Do you think the bank's CEO usually reviews such small applications? This is a waste of my time."

I fold my arms across my stomach. "I'd be happy to speak to one of your lower level loan officers."

"Why?" He stands to match my pose, arms folded

over his chest. "So you can use your succubus wiles to get the loan?"

My mouth drops open in shock. "How dare you!"

"Am I wrong?" He leans across the desk, eyes narrowed. "Where are your sunglasses, Ms. Pond?"

I stab a finger onto my proposal. "This is a sound investment."

"Is it?" Now both eyebrows arch. "You didn't have enough confidence in it to come in ready to deal fairly."

"If you'd planned to reject it from the beginning, you should have refused the meeting." Angry, I reach for the papers on his desk.

His hand flattens on the menu. "I didn't say I would reject it."

My head jerks up. "Excuse me?"

"This is a negotiation, is it not?" The air drops in temperature as his eyes fade to white. "My business partner has a contract already prepared for you."

"I..." My head spins with the sudden victory. "What? You're giving me the loan?"

In answer, he pulls a cellphone from inside his suit jacket and lifts it to his ear. "Please join us."

As he tucks the phone away, blue bleeds back into his eyes, and the air warms slightly. A hidden door next to the bookcase slides open and a tall man enters. Black eyes meet mine from beneath thick eyebrows, and a moment later, the metallic burn of his scent rushes toward me, like calling to like as his energy recognizes itself in my belly.

"Fucking hell."

"Good to see you again, Adeline."

The Offer

I stare at the demon from the coffee shop, legs trembling with the need to bolt.

Has this entire thing been one giant set up? An elaborate trap to harvest my wings?

Feathers move against my spine, ready to burst free and fly me to safety. Only my trim jacket traps them, and even if it didn't, I can't fly. Yet another place where I fail as a succubus.

My eyes drop to the cupcake roses. I can use one of the hard-plastic stems to poke out his eyes. Heat lightning wars with the crackle of ice in the air, and my gaze shifts to the other demon in the room.

Outnumbered. Out powered. Out of luck.

I force my feet to stay planted as the coffee shop demon strides into the room, pulling a wheeled briefcase behind. He walks toward me, one hand extended. “It’s nice to officially meet you. My name is Tobias Braxton. I’m in charge of contracts at K&B Financial.”

“Nice to meet you.” Suspicious, I shake his hand. I drop it quickly and wipe my palm against my skirt to rid myself of the sting left by his touch.

His lips curve with amusement as he watches the gesture. “K&B Financial is ready to fully fund your venture at two hundred percent above what you’re asking for.”

“Excuse me?” I fight down the surge of excitement. “You don’t even know how much I’m asking for.”

“We like to invest in fellow demons.” His eyes crinkle at the corners when he smiles. “It’s our way of encouraging our kind to seek peaceful integration with humans.”

“Okay…” Confused, I glance at Emil, who now sits once more behind his desk, face impassive.

“If you’d like to sign the paperwork now, we can have the check ready at the front desk before you leave today.” Tobias lifts his briefcase onto the desk and opens it to remove a thick stack of papers. “It’s rather long, and full of legal jargon, but I can give you a general overview as we go through it.”

Again, the smile.

My bones ring with warning.

"Thank you." I take the stack from him and sit. "I'll just skim through it first."

"If you have the time." His smile turns tight at the edges. "It will take a few hours to get through the whole thing."

I give him a smile of my own and wave my hand toward the edible roses I assembled for them. "Would you like to sample the cupcakes while you wait? They're delicious."

His dark eyes move to the bouquet, surprised as if he hadn't noticed it before now. While he distractedly investigates the cupcakes, I flip through the papers until my eyes catch on the words *Promissory Note.*

For the value received, the undersigned, Adeline Pond, hereinafter promises to pay in full, as hereinafter provided and upon the following terms and conditions.

Payment will be made on a weekly basis beginning the first week following the date signed on this contract.

Adeline Pond will transfer residence to one of K&B Financial's choosing, where she will reside until such time as the principal sum of one hundred thousand dollars, plus interest, is paid in full.

Interest will compound every fourteen days in the amount of twenty-five percent of the principle owed.

Failure to supply payment will result in a five percent increase in interest—

What was this? Move? Why? And what was with this interest rate?

"What the..." I jerk to my feet. "There's no way this contract is legal. I can't pay over twelve thousand dollars a week off a bakery." I wave the contract at them. "And what's with this demand that I move? I can't afford to move."

Tobias leans a hip against the desk, focus on the cupcake in his hand. "Of course, you can't make that much from selling these things."

"K&B Financial doesn't take monetary reimbursement from our demon clients," Emil adds. An empty wrapper sits next to his elbow, a hint of purple frosting at the corner of his mouth.

Apprehension sinks sharp hooks into me. "What do you take for payment instead?"

Tobias's eyes heat, his voice taking on the burn of volcanos. "Payment is tailored to each demon's specialty."

Succubus only specialize in one thing. "I'm not moving to a whore house! I'm not a prostitute!"

"We'd never ask that, and we're not saying you are," Tobias soothes. "If you keep reading the contract, the payment is in energy draws. If the condition I saw you in yesterday is anything to go by, it actually benefits you to sign. You're obviously incapable of feeding yourself."

I stiffen. "I don't kill humans."

Emil huffs in irritation as he glances at the other man. "This is a waste of time. We need to move on to Plan B."

"Give it time." Tobias waves a hand at him before his attention returns to me. "We're not asking you to feed on humans. As the contract states, you'd move to our residence and pull energy from us. Each draw would equate to five thousand dollars."

"Let me get this straight." I set the contract on the seat behind me before turning back to them, arms folded under my breasts. "You want me to move into your house and pull energy from you every week, and in return, you give me the money to open my bakery."

"There's three of us." Tobias frowns at the small cake in his hand and sets it aside, untasted. "But in very general terms, yes."

I nod slowly. "Okay, well, in very general terms, I

came here for the chance to open a bakery, not to become a whore. So, you can all fuck off."

"You won't get a better offer." Emil straightens in his seat. "In fact, if you want a loan, this is the only offer you'll receive."

I scoff. "There are other banks."

"Not where you're concerned." Tobias's eyes bleed to black, the metallic taste of thunderstorms thick in the air. "It's a good bargain. You should sign."

I shiver, lips parting to drag the scent across my tongue. The meter maid left an empty place in my stomach that wants to be filled. But I don't trust it. The contract leans too far in my favor.

My gain is clear. Where's theirs?

I bend my knees far enough to retrieve my briefcase while keeping my focus on them. "I'm leaving."

Frost crackles along the desk's surface, and the color bleeds from Emil's eyes as he watches my retreat. My pulse spikes with warnings of danger, but all he says is, "You'll come back."

"Not in this lifetime." I reach the door and yank it open. "Enjoy the cupcakes, assholes."

All the way home, I shake with nerves. At this point, I'm pretty sure both Emil and Tobias are high-level demons; the kind that snuff out mid-levels like myself without any effort. How did I manage to draw their attention, and how long will it take for their interest to go elsewhere? The old ones are especially well known for fixating once something catches their attention.

How did my desire to lead a quiet, semi-normal demonic life land me in this situation?

I pull up in front of my apartment complex and climb out, dragging my briefcase along. Its weight drags at my arm. I need to call other banks, try to get a meeting. But Tobias's warning rings in my ear. Does K&B Financial have enough clout to blacklist me from all other banks? Is that even a thing?

Unfortunately, when it comes to demons, it's a real possibility.

I push through the lobby door and stop to pick up my mail before taking the elevator to my floor. When I reach my apartment door, I punch in the code.

The lock buzzes loudly and refuses to open.

With a deep sigh, I punch in the code again.

Buzz!

Again.

Buzz!

What's wrong with the door?

About to try again, a pink slip of paper in the stack of mail catches my attention. Heart pounding with trepidation, I slide it free, eyes catching on the bold, black print at the top.

Eviction Notice.

Persona non Grata

I slam open the door to HelloHell Delivery. "Julian! Get your vinyl covered ass out here, right now!"

Around the office, heads pop up from over cubicle walls, hands-free microphones hanging from their ears. The scent of demonic ozone hangs heavy in the air and skates across my skin like tiny sparklers.

Eyes narrowed, I search for the telltale white curls of my cousin. A flicker of light catches my attention. In the back of the room, a frosted glass door displays the word *management* in gold foil across the front. The office beyond lies suspiciously dark.

As I march toward the door, the pink eviction notice crinkles in one fist. Whispers mark my passing, followed by a frantic shuffle. A low-level demon stumbles into the aisle, arms out to catch himself.

The coworkers who pushed him out in front of

me duck back into hiding, little mice scurrying away from a hungry cat.

I shake my head to drop my sunglasses low on my nose and stare at him over the brim. "Move. Now."

He hunches lower, staring at me from the corner of his eye. "Boss isn't in right now, ma'am."

"The hell he isn't." Through the frosted glass, a darker blur with a hint of red at waist height stands out against the darkness. "Julian, get out here this minute!"

The fuzzy figure darts away from the door.

"P-please, he's not here," the cowering demon insists. "If you'd like to leave a message—"

He stutters to a stop as I lean closer to him, nostrils flaring. He smells like baby powder and mud. Mischief demon. Good for hiding car keys and left socks.

My lip curls with distaste. "Do you want me to eat you, little man? There's a hole in my belly that needs to be filled."

"Please don't!" He squeaks, crouching lower. "I only just got to the human plane."

Guilt and self-disgust slice through me. While my cousins enjoy tormenting lower life forms, it's never been a hobby of mine. His fear sours the air and rolls in my stomach, making me nauseous.

But the threat had the desired effect. I step around his cowering form and storm to the office. How dare Julian not come out instantly to defend his employee.

The doorknob resists my first effort to turn it. Through the door, I hear the scurry of footsteps and a thud.

Spindling out a precious line of energy, I twist it harder, snapping the flimsy lock. My apartment has a code for entry to avoid people entering without my approval. It's a far better locking system. Or, at least it was. Before it was turned against me, locking me out of my own home.

When I throw the door open, the glass rattles in the frame. I pat the wall until I find the light switch.

Julian blinks from his place at the desk on the left side of the room, his feet propped up on his cherry oak surface. "Oh, darling, when did you get here?"

Ignoring his pretense, I wave the pink piece of paper at him. "What the hell is this, Julian?"

His blue eyes dart to my hand, and his mouth forms a moue. "Well, I'd think it was obvious. You didn't need to come all the way down here just for that."

"You kept declining my calls!"

"Yes, I wasn't being subtle." One white eyebrow arches. "Take a hint, darling."

Annoyed, I march forward and toss the crumpled piece of paper on the desk. "This is bullshit. You already cashed my check for this month."

"Well, darling, here's the thing." His feet drop to the ground with a thud as he smooths out the paper to show the bold writing on the front that reads *Eviction Notice*. "You broke the law, so I really had no choice. I have bosses, too, you know."

My mouth drops open in shock, and I snap my teeth closed. "What law?"

"I wasn't told." With one long finger, he nudges the offensive notice back toward me. "The order came this morning from higher up."

My heart lurches. What could I have done to the higher ups? I lean my hands on the desk for support, gaze focused on my cousin. "Julian, that's my home. What am I supposed to do?"

"You better find out who you pissed off, darling, and find out fast." He stands and walks around the desk, red vinyl short-shorts creaking. His fingers curl around my shoulder to turn me around. "But in the meantime, you can't be here."

"What are you talking about?" I stumble as he propels me toward the door.

"You're persona non grata right now." His hand shifts to between my shoulder blades to hurry me along. "I can't be seen with you. I have a business to consider. Employees that rely on me."

I dig in my heels. "Like you care about your employees."

"Well, of course I do." With a grunt, he pushes against me. "They make me money."

I grab onto the doorframe. "What about my stuff?"

"It's going on auction in three days." His shoulder digs into my back, and he forces me out the door.

"Oh, is that little Adie?" A syrupy voice coos from the front of the office.

Julian and I freeze, heads swiveling in unison. A woman stands next to the first cubical in the room, the cowardly demon from earlier tucked against one voluptuous breast. White hair flows straight past her shoulders, the tips crimson red.

"Cassandra," Julian growls, his body stiffening against mine. "To what do I owe the pleasure?"

She licks bright-red lips. "I thought I'd pop in for a bite, see how my cousin is doing."

"Just fine, thank you for coming." Julian launches into action, latching onto my arm and dragging me toward another exit in the back. The door, painted the same dull beige as the rest of the office, blends into the wall.

I hunch my shoulders, suddenly eager to be gone. Cousin Cassandra likes to meddle, and I already have enough on my plate.

"Why the hurry?" She purrs as she stalks forward, dragging the poor demon with her. "I haven't seen little Adie in over a year."

"And you're not seeing her now." Julian waves his hands in front of me in a weaving pattern. "This is a figment of your over-sexed imagination."

"No such thing as over-sexed." Her orange eyes fix on me. "I heard the most delicious rumor on the way over here."

"What rumor?" I demand, the need to know overriding my instincts for self-preservation.

"No. No talking." Julian reaches past me to push open the emergency exit and shoves me through.

I stumble and spin around. "Wait!"

"Solve your own problem, darling," he hisses before the door slams in my face.

Dumbfounded, I stare at the smooth surface, devoid of handle. Damn one-way door. I kick the door in frustration, then swear as it dents the point on my high-heeled shoe.

"Damn you, Julian!" I pound on the door instead,

the solid metal hard against my fist. "Give me back my apartment!"

The concrete walls of the stairwell echoes my pathetic voice back at me. For a moment, my knees tremble with the urge to collapse. After the day I've had, I deserve a nice pity party.

I planned to do just that when I got home. The bottle of wine I set aside to celebrate my loan could just as easily have helped me drown the sense of hopelessness left by my meeting with K&B Financial.

Tobias Braxton's smug face pops to the forefront of my mind, followed closely by the haughty expression of Emil König. Could they be responsible for this recent turn of events?

I replay the meeting, searching my memory for any small laps in my behavior that could have broken a law, no matter how small, in the demon world. With the exception of a few curse words, I left there with less than I took with me. Our meeting ended with the balance in their favor, however little my cupcake bouquet was worth.

It taunts me, though, a flutter at the back of my mind that tells me there's a link. Their demand I move in with them aligns too conveniently with my sudden need for a home.

Steeling my spine with determination, I hurry

down the stairs to the ground floor and exit into the alley between two business buildings. My old sedan waits at the curb, haphazardly parked with the front passenger tire up on the curb. I'm in luck; I didn't get towed while I was inside.

My arm itches, a reminder of my earlier encounter with the meter maid. I so don't need another one of those run-ins this week. I need some alone time with a bottle of rubbing alcohol to eradicate the phone number she wrote on my forearm with permanent marker.

I dig the keys out of my skirt pocket and unlock the driver's side door. As I slide inside, I glance at my briefcase in the passenger seat and freeze. A thick stack of paper stamped with the K&B Financial logo rests neatly on top of the black leather case.

Eyes narrowed, I snatch it up, climb back out of the car, and stomp to the nearest trashcan on the sidewalk, shoving the contract inside. I stare at it, fists opening and closing with frustration.

Yeah, they definitely have something to do with my current situation. I just need to figure out how they managed to do this. If someone is claiming I broke a law, then they would have had to file a claim against me. Which means all I need to do is go to the claims office to find out what law K&B Financial says I broke.

Then I can file a counter claim for harassment.

I smile as I turn back to my car. If they want to play this game, then so be it.

"Now serving number five hundred and twenty-two," the woman at the front desk speaks into the microphone, her monotone voice blaring across the large waiting room. Her impassive gaze travels over the sea of demons, each waiting for their number to come up. When no one immediately leaps from their seat, she presses the microphone button once more and sighs heavily into it. "Now serving number five hundred and twenty-two. Number five hundred and twenty-two."

I double check the ticket in my hand, just in case. *Five hundred and twenty-four.* Nope, not me. After four hours of waiting, I'm ready to call it a day. My ass hurts from the hard seat, my shoulders and neck stiff beyond belief. Unfortunately, I have nowhere else to go.

"Now serving number five hundred and twenty-three."

Three rows up, a lava demon lurches to his feet, charcoal black skin cracked to reveal the molten red glow beneath. The blue plastic chair sticks to his backside, and he peels it off, setting the misshapen piece of furniture back in place before he lumbers toward the front where a clerk waits, safely barricaded behind a thick plate of glass reinforced by metal bars.

Overhead, the number on the reader board changes with a loud click. As the front desk lady resumes her seat, the overhead music comes back on, an even drone of piano that loops every five minutes.

Hell truly is the waiting room of a bureaucratic office.

My neighbor shifts uncomfortably in his seat and huffs with aggravation. His breath wafts over me, smelling of red licorice, and it makes my stomach rumble. While demons don't require as much food as humans do, we still need to give our corporeal forms sustenance. For every hour I go hungry, my body takes more of the energy in my belly.

My gaze shifts from the ticket in my hand to the half eaten box of candy in my neighbor's lap. He reaches into the open wrapper and pulls out a red rope, bringing it to his lips. Saliva floods my mouth as I watch him take a bite. He smiles at me, extending the box in my direction.

With a shake of my head, I force myself to look away. I have nothing to trade for it.

He leans closer, bringing with him the ambiguous allure of red dye 40 and corn syrup. "What are you here for?"

"I need to look someone up on the registry," I respond, not really lying but not telling the whole truth, either. "What about you?"

"Filing a transfer." He taps the box of candy against an envelope that sticks out of his coat pocket. "Wife wants to move north."

"Oh? How long have you been married?" Demon's don't often participate in the human practice of marriage.

Long lives tend to make people twitchy at the idea of being locked together for centuries. Unlike humans, demons take their contracts seriously. Nothing short of murder will break a marriage bond, and most demons don't want to pay the blood price for killing one of our own. Destroying a corporeal body is one thing, but snuffing out another demon's life force…

"Going on two centuries now. We have twenty imps." He reaches into his back pocket to pull out his wallet. With a proud smile, he opens it and a long line of pictures unfolds, the bottom of it hitting the floor and continuing to extend. He points to a gray blob with horns. "This one here is Imperial Rex—"

"Now serving number five hundred and twenty-four."

I leap from my seat and stumble as the blood rushes back to my legs. "That's me!"

With a brief wave, I pick my way to the main aisle, careful not to step on the imp pictures, and head for the front desk. Every step feels like a hundred needles as my feet come back to life. As soon as I sort this mess out, these heels need to go in the trash. Never again, female torture devices.

"I'm number five hundred and twenty-four." I shove my ticket across the desk as proof, and the woman stares down at it for one long moment.

With a slow blink, her gaze shifts to me. "Go to window three."

I bob my head and hurry to the clerk's desk with a large, bronze number three on the front.

The woman stares at me from behind her protective barrier. "How may I help you?"

I crouch to put my mouth close to the narrow opening between the desk and the sheet of glass. "A complaint was filed against me, today. I'd like to know what my offense is."

She taps at her keyboard. "Name?"

"Adeline Pond."

"Middle name?"

Heat fills my cheeks as I whisper, "Boo."

She doesn't even blink at the weird middle name Landon, my mentor, cursed me with during one of his animated movie binges.

After a moment more of typing, she taps her screen. "Adeline Boo Pond is charged with energy poaching in Kellen Maximus Cassius's territory to the equivalent of one human…"

A buzz fills my ears, drowning out the rest of her words. That asshole, he really did it. He actually filed a claim against me for skimming energy at his club last night.

Swan Diving

My tires chirp as I slam to a stop in front of the night club. Overhead, in neon, the word Fulcrum slants upward with a line under it, as if on a teeter-totter. The windows below flash as the strobe lights inside alternate between on and off. Like last night, a line forms at the door.

I climb out, tugging my now wrinkled skirt into place over my knees. My formal business suit stands out among the scantily clad humans ready to get their grind on. I might as well paint loser across my forehead. I stride toward the bouncer at the front entrance, keeping the wince off my face as every step drives spikes of pain into my feet.

"Sorry, toots." The bouncer's arm blocks my path as he stares down at me in disbelief. "You're not getting in tonight looking like that."

Annoyed, I yank open the buttons on my blouse to expose my neon blue bra beneath. "How about now?"

He stares at the milky swell of my breasts, the nipples darker shadows through the bright lace. Slowly, he nods. "Yeah, I can dig the dirty secretary look."

I pat his large chest and stare up at him, careful to keep my powers restrained. My sunglasses remain in the cup holder in my car, and I don't want to risk losing any more energy right now. "Then come find me when your shift ends, yeah?"

"Oh, yeah." His arm drops away.

The couple at the front of the line scowl at me, the woman yelling, "Hey, why does she get to cut?"

"Because her tits are amazing." The bouncer takes one more second to stare before he waves me inside.

"If I show you my boobs, can we speed this up?" The woman's angry voice demands as I walk through the door.

"I can see them from here. They're not getting you inside."

"How dare you!"

The throbbing music drowns them out as I push through the people who loiter in the hall, most with cell phones pressed to one ear and a hand to the other in a desperate attempt to make a phone call without leaving the premises. One leather-clad man shouts into his phone, his face red from either anger or overheating. Leather doesn't breathe very well. Even the shiny fake stuff that hugs his skinny legs.

I skirt around him and duck through the red curtain at his back. Immediately, the music swells louder, the air hot and heavy with perfume and the musky sweat from exertion. Excitement and lust lick along my skin, just waiting to be pulled into my belly to fill the quickly emptying space.

The cheeseburgers I grabbed on the way here did little to curb my hunger. All that wonderful energy I pulled in yesterday barely warms me now, the reserves that should have easily lasted a week depleted to dangerous levels in under twenty-four hours.

Nostrils flaring, I sift through the junk food scents of humanity in search of ozone and thunder clouds. That Kellen guy has to be here. He wouldn't have gone through so much effort to get my attention and then make himself hard to find.

But, like last night, the crowd masks him.

"Hey, baby, love the look," a man shouts as he shimmies up to me. Through his mesh shirt, silver studs wink from his nipples. "Dance with me!"

"No." I push past him, aiming for the back hall where Kellen took me last night.

By the time I get there, my open blouse clings to my skin, sticky with other people's sweat. A good succubus would be out there reveling in the press of so much exposed skin. But tonight, it grosses me out.

I want a bath. With bubbles. Preferably pink ones that smell like cotton candy.

Anger spikes anew. No expensive bubble bath for me. It's locked out of reach by this asshole demon who can't admit defeat with grace.

The bright lights of the hallway reveal two doorways. I march to the first and fling it open, startling a pair of humans inside who sit at a round table. A fridge and sink take up one side of the room, with a filtered water dispenser shoved in the corner. A break room.

A man in one of the club's black uniform t-shirt's drops his half eaten sandwich and stands. "Hey, you can't be back here."

I focus on him. "Where's Kellen?"

"Who? No one here goes by that name." He scoots around the narrow space to stand in front of his fellow employee. Unlike the bouncer, this one seems to take my exposed chest as a threat. "You drunk? Need me to call you a cab?"

Eyes narrowing, I blink slowly. I'm not wrong, am I? This is the only place I've skimmed energy from lately. I practically starved myself to death locked up in my apartment for an entire month while I got the plans together for my bakery. And before that, I only went out with the cousins to demon approved feeding grounds or did ride-alongs to Dreamland.

My wings shift beneath my skin, a mild grate of irritation against my spine. "Tall, sexy as fuck, red hair." I hold my hands up, about two and a half feet apart. "Shoulders like this."

He straightens with recognition, and his gaze becomes even more weary. "Oh, you must mean Mr. Cassius. He doesn't see people without an appointment." He reaches into his back pocket and pulls out a business card, passing it over. "Try calling in the morning."

His doubtful tone tells me he expects my call to be shuffled off. I must not be the first deranged woman to come hunting his boss. Snapping the card out of his hand, I tuck it into the cup of my bra where its hard edges poke against my breast.

"Is he here tonight?" As the man's shoulders stiffen, I smile. Answer enough for me. Kellen's here somewhere. "Thanks."

I close the door and shove down hard on the

handle, bending it far enough to lock them inside. Can't risk them following to escort me from the premise before I find Kellen. Humans can be meddlesome.

I check the second door at the end of the hall, unsurprised to find the management office dark and empty.

Back out on the dance floor, I search the sea of bobbing heads for one in particular, but find it impossible to distinguish features through the strobe lights. Pushing my way through the dancers, energy prickles across my skin like firecrackers. The temptation to suck it in almost overwhelms me.

I wiggle away from the hungry grasp of hands and make my way to the DJ booth. A thick, red rope cordons off the square platform. With no security in sight, I duck under the paltry barrier and walk around to the back, where a short flight of stairs leads up.

The DJ casts me a startled glance as I join him at the top. He yanks off one side of his headphones and covers the microphone. "You can't be up here."

"I'm just taking a look." I stare out over the crowd, locating a VIP section on one side, close to the bar. But none of the occupants have Kellen's distinctive red hair.

"You need to leave." The DJ waves an arm, and

one of the security guards peels away from the dance floor, creating a wide path as he shoulders his way through the crowd.

For an odd moment, as the song transitions, everyone on the dance floor freezes and a glyph glows across their still forms. The light forms two swirling storm clouds with a third folding back on itself. Freezing in place, my eyes lift to the balcony over the front entrance where Kellen's mark glows on the wall, obvious now for anyone who knows what to look for. The source of that prickly energy I felt, stinging against my skin. Last night, I would have known what it meant and left immediately. But it hadn't been active last night.

Kellen, backlit by his demon mark, grips the railing and stares across the dance floor at me. Beside him, Tobias's arms drape over the rail as he slouches next to Emil who stands rigidly at his side. Kellen's arm extends toward me, fingers curling to beckon me to them.

For a moment, the temptation they present shakes my resolve. An unlimited buffet for me to lose myself in. Giving in now means never being hungry again. My belly aches to be filled. But then the platform shakes as the security guard reaches the DJ booth, his feet heavy on the temporary stairs as he stomps up them.

I snap back to reality. Adeline Boo Pond will not be owned. Even by such scrumptious man candy.

Arms lifting, I pop my middle fingers up at them in the universal sign language of *Not today, assholes.*

Kicking off my high heels, I chuck them at the security guy's head, then climb onto the narrow ledge of the DJ booth and swan dive into the crowd below.

I keep a white-knuckled grip on the steering wheel all the way out of town. My foot on the gas twitches, and I glance at the speedometer to make sure the needle stays perfectly at fifty-five.

Somewhere in the crush of dancers, I lost my shirt, and getting pulled over by the human police right now, low on energy and half naked, would be the icing on the cake of my horrible day.

Luckily, the cell phone strapped in my thigh holster made it through the gropes of hundreds of hands, and I was able to call Landon when I got back outside.

Either he hasn't heard about my situation, or he

has nothing to lose by allowing me to crash at his place tonight.

Spotting the neon-orange rooster, I pull off the dark highway and into the drive-thru of Bucket-O-Wings. Only one car, probably an employee's, sits in the over-bright parking lot. Rolling down my window, I slow to a stop at the speaker.

It hisses with static, and a bored voice comes through. "Bucket-O-Wings, where life tastes better deep fried. How may I help you?"

I lean out the window. "I'd like two twelve-piece buckets, six biscuits, and a large potato salad, please."

"Crispy, extra-crispy, or crispy-supreme?"

"Crispy-supreme." Landon likes an equal amount of breading to meat ratio.

"Will that be all?"

Nibbling my lip, I scan the menu. "Do you have any of the strawberry cheesecake pies?"

"One, moment." The speaker hiss cuts off, and a full minute ticks by before he comes back. "We have apple or custard pie."

Shoulders drooping, my nose and eyes sting as I fight back tears.

My bare feet hurt against the car pedals, I'm sticky, and I'm pretty sure the sour stench that keeps wafting past my nose comes from somewhere on my body. Not getting my favorite fast food dessert is the final straw in my horrible day. I can't deal anymore.

I slump back in my car.

"Ma'am?" The bored voice sounds more impatient now. "Did you want the apple or custard pie?"

I sniffle and wipe my nose with the back of my hand. "Custard, please."

"Ma'am? I didn't catch that."

I lean back out the window. "Custard pie, please!"

I don't even like custard pie, but I'm getting dessert, damnit!

"That will be fifty-three twenty-five at the first window."

At the window, I hand over my credit card, ignoring the gawking stare of the pimple-faced teenager as he ogles my boobs.

"You having a good night, ma'am?" he asks as he passes back my card.

"No, not at all." I shove it back into my wallet and throw it in the passenger seat.

"You just come from a party?" He holds out three large bags of food, the sides bulging. As I twist to put them in the passenger seat, his voice rises with sudden excitement. "Or are you on your way to one? Can I come?"

"Nope." I roll up my window before he can ask

any more questions and pull away from the window, one hand searching in the bags for my box of pie.

By the time I pull into Landon's driveway and climb out of my car, sweet custard coats my tongue and my spirits feel brighter, artificially lifted by the sugar boost. Who said food can't cure problems? Even my belly feels less hollow.

Juggling the fast food bags, I push open Landon's front door. Plastic bottles roll down the hallway, pushed into motion by my entrance, and I kick more out of the way to close and lock the door behind me. Landon might not worry about security, but with the day I just survived, I want the extra precautions against intruders.

"That you, Boo?" Landon yells from the back of the house.

"I brought food." Careful of where I step, I follow the sound of gunfire and explosions.

Landon's horde of discarded water bottles covers the floor, accumulated over the last month while I worked on my business plans instead of coming over to clean for him. Empty cardboard crates line one side of the hall, interspersed with stacks of old pizza boxes.

The scent of fresh, clean greenery adds an odd counterpoint to the mess. I squint as I walk into the kitchen, bright with indoor grow-lights. The blue tips of my hair lift on a gentle breeze, bringing with it the cleansing sweetness of violets and golden rods.

Potted plants cover every available surface, lush greens with pops of vibrant flowers. Stone fountains burble throughout the room, adding to the sense of an outdoor garden.

Vibrant colored wings flutter as I disrupt the butterflies, and dozens of the jeweled bugs fly into the air to swarm around my head. Annoyed, I swat them away. Stupid creatures should go into hiding at the first hint of demon. Instead, they seem drawn to our scent like moths to a flame.

Some demons, and I shudder to think of it as I flick an especially persistent blue one away, like to eat butterflies. Their small life-force feels like pop rocks on the tongue.

Gross.

An enormous, flat-screen television illuminates the living room and the mummified demon who hunches on the couch, tapping away at his game controller. How Landon finds time to tend to his butterfly garden, but not go into Dreamland to feed himself, I will never understand. Demon needs to get his priorities straight.

"Here's your food."

"Thanks, Boo," he grunts, eyes fixated on the

screen. "You bring me some energy, too? I'm pretty hard up right now."

"Then go into Dreamland, stupid." I brush more empty water bottles off the other side of the couch and curl into the corner, body sore and ready to sleep. "There has to be some of your usual contacts taking a nap."

"Not until they reach level fifty in *Hell & Heaven*. My feeders are hardcore." He glances at me and frowns before his attention returns to the game. "I like the slut look. You finally making connections on the human plane?"

"Shut up." I tug the blanket off the back of the couch and pull it around my shoulders. Next, I snag a pillow off the floor and wedge it against my stomach. Its lumpy stuffing doesn't sooth me the way my purple-sequined pillow does. I study Landon's profile, ruggedly handsome even in starvation. "Hey, do you know a demon named Kellen Maximus Cassius?"

Landon fumbles his game controller, and online, his half-naked elf soldier takes a headshot. His head turns far enough for me to glimpse the sunken hollow of his Monarch-yellow eyes. "No clue."

Liar. But past experience tells me that when he doesn't want to talk about it, no amount of nagging will sway him. With a sigh, I hug the pillow closer to my belly. "Thanks for letting me stay the night."

"Anytime, Boo." Distracted, he reaches for a piece of fried chicken. "Besides, you're feeding me."

"Yeah." Knees against my chest, I wrap my arms around them. I miss my pile of pillows at home. But at least I can always come back to my mentor.

(UN)EXPECTED

"Boo, wake up."

I groan as Landon shakes my shoulder. "What time is it?"

"Just after eight am." He shakes me again. "Get up."

"Go away." My whole body aches, skin tight and itchy. Shivering, I huddle closer around my lumpy pillow, kick weakly at him, and connect with a solid thigh.

With a grunt, his hand disappears from my shoulder. In the next instant, he yanks my blanket off. Wound up inside of it, I fly off the couch and pain explodes through my body as I hit the coffee table, then land on the floor. Empty water bottles rain down on top of me, adding insult to injury.

I lurch to my hands and knees, glaring around blearily until I find Landon on the opposite side of the room, out of range. Even with only the television's light to see by, he appears healthier, the hollows of his face filled in. His matted white hair from earlier now glows with vitality.

My eyes drop to my skeletal arms, covered in skin that resembles paper mache. "Damnit, asshole, you took too much!"

He holds up his hands in self-defense. "I'm sorry, I was distracted while I skimmed you."

"Do you know how hard it is for me to fill up?" My wings rustle against my spine, ready to spring forth as I stare at all that stolen energy rolling around inside of him. "I'm going to eat you down to dust and bone."

He snaps straight and points at me. "Okay, one, no you're not, so keep those wings sheathed. I have hundreds of years on you, Boo." He points at the kitchen. "And, two, there's a meal waiting for you in the other room, which is why I woke you up."

Vertebra popping, my head swivels, and I blink at the bright kitchen. My attention returns to him. "What are you talking about?"

For the first time, I notice the television's black screen, a sure sign his gaming system sat on pause long enough to lapse into sleep mode. But he doesn't glow with enough energy inside to indicate he actually went hunting in Dreamland while I slept.

He flicks the blanket at me, and I flinch back. "To the kitchen with you. I have people to kill and biscuits to eat."

Painfully, I climb to my feet, kicking empty chicken buckets out of the way. The box of biscuits sits in the center of the coffee table next to a bowl of potato salad, the plastic spork sticking up from the center like a flag pole.

My stomach growls, but not with the desire for human food. Landon drained out every spark of energy I managed to glean yesterday, leaving me back at square one. As I turn toward the kitchen, the jeweled flutter of butterfly wings draws my eyes, and I shudder with disgust, fingers already twitchy to catch the repulsive bugs.

Resigned, I march toward them. "I'm never bringing you food again."

"Don't say that, Boo." The couch creaks as Landon resumes his seat. "No one else cleans up after me."

Blue wings flutter in front of my face, one of Landon's more prized creations. It struggles as I form a loose cage around it with my fingers, the black tips of its wings ticklish against my palms. My stomach rolls. I really don't want to eat it, but its energy warms my cold hands, a small precursor to the warmth that will suffuse my body once I suck its tiny life force away.

As I bring my cupped hands up to my mouth, a throat clears to my right. Jumping, I spin to face the kitchen table, releasing the butterfly. Instead of escaping, the stupid thing flutters back in front of my face to be caught again. I swat it away and stare at the demon in Landon's kitchen.

Emil König sits at Landon's chintzy kitchen table, a blight among all the greenery as the frost from his skin creeps across the potted plants nearby. Frozen butterflies lay on the ground next to his polished black loafers. Landon must get the same danger warnings from this demon that I do; otherwise, he would already have chased Emil from the house.

I narrow my eyes at him. "Mr. König, how unexpected."

He straightens the cuffs on his black suit jacket. "Sarcasm is the lowest form of humor, Miss Pond."

"Then, please, find me unbearable and leave." I rub the goose bumps on my arms and shiver, wishing for the thin warmth of the couch blanket.

Emil's bright-blue eyes flicker over me. "I see

Kellen was correct in his assessment of your inability to feed yourself."

"I'm very troublesome." I bare my teeth at him. "Far too bothersome for someone like you."

"Have you given up on the bakery idea then?" He arches one translucent eyebrow as he reminds me of his hold over my prospective loan. "It's a silly idea, anyway. Obviously something you're not suited for."

"Oh?" Anger spikes through me as I step toward him, the tiles cold beneath my bare toes. "And you know so much about what I'm suited for?"

He leans back in his chair, knees spread wide as if he sits behind his desk at the bank, ruler of his kingdom. "If you can't even take care of yourself, why would I think you can take care of a business? You're a succubus, it can't be that hard to feed."

"You know nothing about me." Gaze dropping to his mouth, I lick my lips.

The closer I get, the more his unique scent of crisp, fresh snowfall tickles my nose. Far more alluring than the butterflies. I shiver, this time with more than cold.

He leans his chin in his hand, pinkie curled next to his lips as he watches my approach. "Are you hungry, Adeline?"

Frost melts beneath my toes as I freeze in front of

him, jerking my eyes up to meet his. "What did you come here for?"

His knees slowly close until he boxes in my legs, a venus flytrap catching its prey. "You seem to keep misplacing your contract, so I brought you a new one."

The chill of his body creeps into my bones to form ice crystals in my blood, making me feel slow and heavy. "Isn't that going above and beyond, Mr. Bank President?"

"You also left this at the club." He reaches through two potted plants to pull out a soiled rag of material.

Confused, I stare at it for a moment before recognition sets in. My blouse. Then my gaze jerks to my lace-covered breasts, inches from the man's face. His attention shifts, too, and the temperature drops until his body becomes so cold it burns where his legs touch mine. Instead of hurting, it fills me with a melting heat and an overwhelming desire to curl into his lap to sleep.

My bones rattle with danger, shaking me out of the lassitude.

"You didn't have to bring it here personally." I reach for the blouse, and he drops it to curl his fingers around my wrist.

"What's this?" He rotates my arm to show the underside where the meter maid wrote her number in black sharpie.

Usually, I don't feed on humans. It's so hard to only take a little of their life energy while corporeal. But if I'm very careful, I won't hurt her. And I'll only have to put up with her bondage kink this one time. While I don't like to be tied up, starvation wins over squeamishness this time. Of course, Landon didn't leave me with any energy to beguile her. Will my whammy from yesterday still cloud her perception?

I shrug. "Breakfast, maybe."

When I tug on my arm, his grip tightens. "There's no need to dine out when I'm already here."

"I'm not signing that contract." I search the table for the offensive stack of papers, but he stashed it out of sight.

His other hand lifts to my bare waist. "Call it an advance."

"Get your ears fixed. I'm not signing." I shiver as his thumb traces patterns next to my belly button, little circles from which hunger spirals outward. My pulse spikes, rushing blood to all the good places in my body.

Cold breath puffs across my breast, and my nipple

tightens into a hard pebble. Emil glances up at me through white eyelashes. "Then pay me."

I stiffen my spine to stop myself from swaying toward his mouth, only inches away. Will his tongue be cold like the rest of him? Will he taste of icicles? I shake my head. "I don't have any cash."

He frowns with distaste. "I don't need money." His grip on my wrist shifts, his fingers gliding over the black numbers on my arm. "Give me this."

"The meter maid?" Unable to resist temptation, my free hand lifts, fingers sifting through the stiff strands of hair at the back of his neck. "What will you do with her?"

His palm slides up to the bottom of my rib cage. "Does it matter?"

I freeze in place, and my pulse slows as I stare down at him. "Yes. It does actually."

He leans back, taking his tempting mouth away from me. "Why? Weren't you going to suck her dry anyway?"

Now *I* lean away from *him*, the bracket of his knees against the back of mine preventing me from going farther. "As I said before, you know nothing about me."

"I've met enough succubi to know your kind."

"Then go harass one of them." Annoyed, I twist

within his trap, offended at his claim to know more of my kind. Of course he would. His obvious power means he's old, even among demons.

"I only want the number." He yanks me forward to sprawl against his chest. This close, his energy stings against my skin like frostbite. Our noses touch, his mouth a breath away from mine. "Is it a deal?"

Resisting temptation, I push for more. "How much is the number worth to you?"

Amusement flickers through his eyes. "Just don't drain me dry."

I don't wait for him to change his mind. My arms wind around his neck, my mouth fastening over his. When he doesn't open fast enough, I catch his bottom lip between my teeth and tug, then sweep my tongue across his teeth.

My fingers dig into his hair, making a mess of his careful business style. I fist my hands in the thick strands and yank his head back, satisfied when he grunts and his mouth opens for me.

His tongue does taste like icicles, metallic and mineral, and my lips grow numb. Uncaring, I lap at the energy that fills him, so much that it practically spills down my throat faster than I can swallow it. Ice tea on a hot summer day. Invigorating. As it floods into my belly, my body sings with renewed life.

"Hey, that looks delicious. Mind if I top off?" Landon calls from the doorway.

I yank back, twisting to hiss at my mentor. Emil is *my* food source.

Landon holds up his hands in surrender. "Whatever, just clean up when you're done."

Snatching a butterfly from the air, he ambles back out of the kitchen.

Mortified, I stare at the empty space where he stood. Never once have I hissed at Landon.

"You're not done already, are you?" Emil rumbles from beneath me.

Startled, I turn back to him. My legs wind around him, ankles locked around the back of the chair, my arms looped around his neck like he's some kind of tree I'm trying to climb.

He studies my face for a moment. "Take more. By my calculation, I've only paid for six of the numbers so far."

Julian would charge me a small fortune for what I already took. "Remind me not to ask you for investment advice."

His hands smooth up my back, over the place where my wings shift restlessly beneath my skin, and he urges me closer. "One more sip should do it."

I stiffen with apprehension. "Why are you so eager for me to take your energy?"

His eyebrows lift. "Didn't we agree on a price?"

"No, actually, we didn't." Slowly, I unwind my legs. "That's rather clumsy for a business man."

He scowls. "I said not to drain me dry."

"That's like writing a blank check for a succubus." I push his arms away and climb off his lap, confused all over again by this demon. "Since you know so many of us, you should know not to say something so stupid. I could have destroyed your corporeal form without draining you dry."

He shrugs. "I can always make a new one."

Irritation floods through me in an instant. Not every demon has that luxury. It took me over half a century, and I rushed the job, which lead to my recent issues with re-entering Dreamland. As in, my complete inability to access it.

"Well goody for you." I reach past him to snatch my blouse off the table. "If you're so desperate to get rid of more energy, there's a game obsessed incubus in the other room that will be happy to take care of that for you."

"Now, wait a minute." He jumps to his feet, reaching for my arm.

"No touchie." I swat him away, surprised to find

his hand somewhat warm to the touch. The vein in his forehead throbs in obvious irritation, but the room remains at its climate controlled temperature, not a hint of frost in sight.

He folds his arms across his chest. "I didn't come here to feed your playmate."

"Why did you come?" I shrug into my soiled blouse, ignoring the stench of stale booze that wafts from it.

"I already told you." His eyes lose some of their color, but nowhere near the white they transformed into yesterday. I must have taken more than I realized if his iciness is on the fritz now. "I came to redeliver the contract."

I roll my eyes. "Well you can take it and shove it—"

"Miss Pond!"

"—in the trash." When I discover the majority of the buttons gone from my blouse, I decide to just tie the ends together. I glance at him from the corner of my eye. "Fucking prude."

This time, frost crackles across the floor, quickly spreading toward me.

I back my way to the front door, yelling, "Later, Landon!"

Emil stalks after me the entire way, fog rolling

outward from him with every step. "We're not finished with our discussion."

"We are for now." Using my new energy to increase my speed, I zip out the door and into my car.

It comes to life just as Emil makes it to the porch. Backing around the black sports car that blocks the driveway, I roll down my window, grab the new contract that sits in the passenger seat, and chuck it on the hood of his fancy ride. Then, I peel away like the demons from hell are on my heels.

Because, for some unknown reason, they are.

The Deal

Less than five minutes after leaving Landon's, I pull back into the Bucket-O-Wings drive-thru and order myself a vanilla ice cream cone, ignoring what brought on the sudden craving for a cold treat.

So what if I want to numb my tongue by licking a phallic shaped tower of frozen cream. It has nothing to do with the sexy, annoying demon I left in the driveway.

Sugar cone in hand, I circle around the stucco building and park to eat and figure out what to do next. My current method of running away from the persistent trio won't work forever. It seems their determination will out last my ability to do without basic human needs like a bed and shower.

All of my worldly possessions will be put up for auction in—I check the time on my phone—thirty-six hours. While I might be able to do without most of it, the specialty baking pans and my espresso machine took half a year to buy and my bank account sits dangerously close to zero, with my credit cards near maxed out.

Staring out the windshield at the giant, orange chicken sign, I take a long lick off the ice cream cone.

Not having to pay for the apartment every month really would help out.

Another lick.

Having a ready source of energy wouldn't be a bad deal, either.

My thighs tingle with the half remembered press of Emil's slacks against my bare skin. I'd been too hungry to really appreciate the body of the man I wrapped myself around. Muscular, definitely. Hard…everywhere. And as long as he had something else to do with his mouth besides talk, he was tolerable to be around.

Tobias, too, seems bearable to be around. Though his cocky attitude needs to come down a few pegs. And his obsession with my wings still worries me.

I bite off the top of my ice cream, my throat freezing as I swallow it down.

Kellen, though…he took my home. Helped the others drive me into a corner. How does a club owner fit with the banker duo? Is it just a group of old demons hanging out together? Like one of those good-old-boys clubs?

Lifting my phone from my lap, I tap in the passcode that lets me access the demon registration database. When I type Kellen's name into the city registry, the listing shows him as the owner of Fulcrum Night Club. Not surprising. What shocks me is the long list of other properties he owns, including The Atlas, my mid-rent apartment building.

Anger spikes through me, my fingers tightening on the sugar cone until it cracks down one side. Everything that happened in the last two days feels like some elaborate trap I stumbled into.

But why do they want me so much? Or is it even me they really want? If another succubus had been stupid enough to catch their attention, would I now have my bank loan and be happily on my way to opening my bakery?

Annoyance buzzes through me. I don't like to be the most convenient succubus on hand for their game.

I suck up the last bit of my icy treat, then drop the broken cone into the little trashcan I keep in the car and wipe the stickiness off of my hand with a napkin from the glove box.

Time to go on the offensive.

Back at the clerk's office, I bypass the waiting area where I spent an eternity yesterday and head deeper into in the labyrinth of hallways to the demon library. The closed double-doors discourage visitors, but I press the intercom button on the box mounted to the wall anyway.

After a solid minute passes, I press it again.

It crackles to life, and an irritated voice barks, "What do you want?"

I lean closer to the microphone. "I'd like access to the demon histories, please."

"Do you have a library card?"

"I do." I dig in my wallet and pull it out, then hesitate, unsure what to do with it.

The only other time I came here was with my cousin Cassandra, and the doors were open when we arrived. Did I come outside normal business time? No helpful sign on the wall gives me their normal hours of operation, but they should be open in the morning during the week. My search for a camera comes up empty, so I settle for waving it in front of the microphone box.

The intercom crackles again. "Are you going to scan it, or just leave me hanging in suspense?"

"Umm…" I press the card against the front of the box and move it back and forth. "Did you get it?"

"Oh, for the love of—"

After a moment, the left door pops open and a wizened, old hag zooms forth on a two-wheeled scooter, claws curled around the cheery-red handle bars. Her wrinkled lids droop over her eyes, obscuring them completely as she speeds toward me. I resist the urge to scramble back. That would be beyond rude, and I can't risk offending the library's gatekeeper.

She screeches to a hard stop next to me and extends one hand in expectation. Hurriedly, I hand over the library card, careful of her razor sharp nails.

"You scan it like this." She pinches the card between her middle and foreclaw and flips it over, waving it beneath the intercom, where a red light flicks on. A moment later, it beeps.

"Thank you." Feeling foolish, I take the card back and return it to my wallet.

Her long, pointed nose twitches. "You need a bath, girl. I'm not sure I should let you into my sanctuary."

Blood rushes to my face at the criticism. Emil's apparent disregard for my appearance let me forget for a moment that I last showered yesterday morning, and my clothes are worse for wear.

My bare toes curl against the low-pile carpet in an attempt to hide as I finger-comb my hair in a futile attempt to look more presentable. "I'm sorry. I've recently found myself homeless. This is all I have."

Her wrinkled face tightens into a scowl. "You can't sleep at my library."

"No, I wouldn't do that." I push back the self pity that tries to swamp me with doubt. "I just need to look up a couple demons. They might not even be in the history books."

Her head tilts at an unnatural right angle. "Do you know their names?"

"I know what they go by right now." Demon names are tricky things, evolving and changing over time as they assume different corporeal forms. "Kellen Maximus Cassius, Emil König, and Tobias Braxton."

Her head tilts the other way and a sense of being studied washes over me, as if she can somehow see beneath my skin to the core of what makes me a succubus. "They're a troublesome lot. You should steer clear of them."

I straighten in surprise. "You know them?"

"It's hard not to, when you've lived as long as I have." Her claws tighten on her handlebars, and the scooter spins in a perfect circle. "Don't get mixed up with them. They'll only cause you hardship."

I run behind as she zips back toward the open library door. "I'm already in trouble with them. They won't leave me alone."

"Ah, they must need a new succubus."

I stumble as I pass through the entrance into deep shadows. "What do you mean a *new* succubus?"

My voice sounds muffled in the larger space, far bigger than I remembered from my last visit. When I came before, the library resembled any other modern, human library with short bookcases and bright lights. Now, the rows of computer tables are replaced with bookshelves that tower up to the vaulted ceiling, disproportionate to distance between this room and the city street above. Dim sconces fill the room with more shadow than light.

I glance back at the doorway, searching for the telltale shimmer of a dimensional portal. Pale yellow light rims the entrance on this side. Unnerved, I hurry to the front desk.

The hag's scooter blocks one end where she parked it to lean against the counter. She shuffles behind the desk, only her head visible, until she reaches an ancient computer at the other end. With loud grunts, she climbs up onto the stool in front of it and pulls out a keyboard, attached to the computer by an old, spiral cord.

Eager to find someone with possible answers, I grip the edge of the desk and repeat my question. "What do you mean they need a *new* succubus?"

Her head swivels into another unnatural angle so she faces me straight on while her body stays in place. "You really have no clue who you're dealing with, do you?"

I shake my head. "Their corporeal forms look human. And they don't smell like demons I've met before."

"No, I don't imagine they do!" Her jaw unhinges and a cackle of glee spills across her black tongue. "Run away while you still can. You're centuries too young to play with these three."

My knuckles turn white as I grip the counter. "I won't be driven out of town. Either tell me what you know, or I'll find the information myself."

"Confident, aren't you?" Her talons stab at the keyboard and a low hum fills the room. A moment later, she reaches beneath the counter and pulls out a sheet of paper. "You'll want to reference these volumes."

Taking the list, I point at the high bookcases at my back. "So, I'll find these in there?"

She sighs heavily. "They're numbered. Just follow the plaques."

I check the number listed beside the first book title and walk over to the nearest bookcase to check the numbers on a bronze plate attached to the side. Nowhere near close. Shoulders squared, I march down the long line of books to the next row deeper within the library.

Fifteen minutes later, I find the right bookcase and the volume located on the bottom shelf. Thick and heavy, I drag it onto the floor and sit next to it, tucking my cold toes beneath my knees.

The blank leather cover gives no hint to the book's contents. When I open it, the spine creaks, stiff from disuse. A demon's glyph cuts into the inside cover, pale with age but still legible. Two swirling storm clouds, with a third folding back on itself.

My heart accelerates, excitement making my fingers shake. This is it. An entire volume filled with info about Kellen. Careful, I turn the brittle pages until I find writing.

In a language I don't understand.

The pale scratches that fill the pages in vertical lines look like tally marks, the line height and number of marks varying with an infrequent dot here and there, seemingly thrown in more for aesthetics than to delineate sentence breaks.

Shoulders slumping, I keep turning the pages in hope that, at some point, the language will transition into something legible. Instead, I come across a picture. One of those old style kind that were carved into wood, inked, then pressed onto the page.

It depicts a storm cloud, with a lightning bolt zig zagging down to the ground. A figure stands at the center, arms raised to the sky. Even with the faded details of the image, the demon's face roughly resembles Kellen.

I flip through another two dozen pages before I find the next picture. A tidal wave curves toward a small village, greedy to engulf it and drag the huts and their inhabitants out to sea. Black clouds roll overhead, the etching of a man at the center of them.

The next image I find steps away from the block art and into the fine details of pencil. The artist beautifully detailed the twisting destruction of a tornado as it decimates a small city. And once more, Kellen's figure stands at its center. Always within the storm.

Slowly, I close the book and stare at the cover. While I can't read the damn thing, the pictures and the memory of Kellen's metallic scent of thunderstorms helps to fill in the blanks. He's some kind of Fulgar Demon, someone whose power affects storms, the kind that destroys cities when left out of control.

In the old days, when entire towns could vanish without notice, demons like Kellen were left unsupervised. But as technology advanced, such destruction couldn't continue, not at the frequency the Fulgar Demon's indulged in. Most were banished to the demon realm, corporeal forms forbidden to them on the human plane.

That Kellen walks around free right now means he's taken precautions to subvert his destructive behavior.

I wedge the book back in place and push to my feet, walking to the next one on the list. When I locate it and pull the heavy volume off the shelf, I crack it open to find another glyph etched into the inside cover. This one resembles two inverted *V's* nested together with a horizontal line struck through them. Almost like a partially formed snowflake.

When I turn the pages, I'm unsurprised to find more indecipherable writing and pictures dispersed throughout of frozen landscapes, glacial freezes, and one black image with several moon cycles forming the border in what I can only guess is a depiction of endless night.

The flavor of icicles fills my mouth. Emil, the Eis Demon. Capable of bringing on another ice age. My hands shake as I return the book to its place on the shelf. I argued with him this morning, probably dented the hood of his car when I threw the contract onto it. Being near him, my bones rang with danger, and rightly so.

My feet feel heavy as I force myself to follow the book lined path to the last destination, the volume that will reveal Tobias's origin. This one weighs more, its thick spine almost twice the width of the other two. I open the cover to stare at the glyph, swirling lines with sharp edges that twist together to form a pinwheel.

I flip through the book quickly, searching for the pictures. I find storms, volcanic eruptions, fissures in the ground and crumbling buildings, likely an earthquake.

Confused, I keep turning pages. Unlike the first two, his doesn't seem to center around a specific element. Just natural disasters, one after the other. A few of the images even repeat some of the ones from Emil's and Kellen's books. At the back, a final image shows a forest in mid collapse, the trees on one side tilted over, like dominos taking out the ones in front of it.

I straighten in sudden realization. A Catalyst Demon. His mere presence sets events in motion. Like our chance encounter at the coffee shop that led us to our current standoff.

Quickly, I stride back to the front desk to find the hag clicking away at an ancient game of mah-jongg on her computer screen. Her head swivels around to face me. "Are you properly terrified now?"

"Not at all." I lean against the desk to contain my excitement. "Do you have books on contracts?"

With a smile full of sharp teeth, she lifts another piece of paper from beneath the counter, a list of books already printed on it.

When I pull up to a large house early the next morning, my legs jitter with tension. I fumble the keys twice before placing them in my briefcase, the same one I took to my meeting with the bank only three days ago. The timeline to prevent my worldly possessions from going up for sale draws closer with every tick of the clock, but I needed the extra time to make sure I organized all of the paperwork correctly.

Gathering my briefcase and the tray of coffees I picked up from a drive-thru, I climb out of my old car.

For a moment, nerves get the better of me as I stare at the enormous house. Not technically a mansion, but the two towers, one on either side, definitely give it a feeling of magnificence. A large garage peeks from around the corner, a more modern building that attempts to disguise its function with old world, imitation-barn doors.

A porch wraps around the front of the house, with slender white columns that support the roof overhang. Squaring my shoulders, I march up the steps and use the brass lion head on the door to knock loudly and without pause.

With the sun only a gentle blush on the skyline, I figure the guys need some extra motivation to get their asses out of bed.

The door flies open, the brass knocker ripped from my hand, and an angry Tobias glares out at me. His chestnut-brown waves poof around his head, and the sweatpants he wears hang low on his hips, the tie loose as if he just pulled them on. Far too mouth wateringly delicious for so early in the morning.

"Morning, sunshine!" I smile and shove the tray of coffees against his bare chest.

When he stares at them in dumb confusion, I push past him and step into the rustic foyer. A short bench with a coat rack above and shoes tucked neatly beneath sits off to one side. I rub one bare foot on top of the other, dirt slippery beneath my toes. Not much I can do about the grime, though, since I've been locked out of my apartment and didn't have time to shower at Landon's house.

Cupping my hand next to my mouth, I call, "Honeys, I'm home!"

Quietly, the door closes behind me, and I try not to picture myself as the fly caught in their web. Determined, I square my shoulders and remind myself that I'm the spider now.

This is my trap.

The ceiling creaks overhead, and I follow the sound into a spacious living room that must run the length of the house. A black leather couch face two matched arm chairs with a large coffee table in the middle. Very manly.

Across the room, two flights of stairs, one on either side of an enormous fireplace, curve upward. The creaks in the ceiling gravitate toward them, and soon Emil and Kellen appear at the bottom, both rumpled and confused.

Emil spots me first and makes an attempt to

smooth down his hair which, without the gel, flops across his forehead to make him seem younger. When Kellen's sleepy gaze lands on me, he gives a lazy smile. Unlike the other two, he didn't bother with sweats and his boxer-briefs hug his muscular thighs and perfectly outline his morning wood.

He props his hands on his hips, gaze taking in my ragged appearance. "Well, well. Did you come to sign your contract?"

"Not on your life." I circle the room until I have all three of them in my sight, then raise my briefcase. "I've come to make a deal."

The Terms

My announcement doesn't garner the immediate reaction I hoped for. Instead, Kellen yawns and shuffles to one of the couches to sprawl across it, one leg hanging off the side, foot still on the ground. It perfectly displays the long line of his delicious body and puts the ridged bulge in his boxer briefs on full display.

Emil ignores me, head lifting as he sniffs the air before his ice-colored eyes land on the tray in Tobias's hands. "Is that coffee?"

Tobias grunts in response. "She didn't bring a straw."

"Stay away from mine, Emil," Kellen warns as he folds an arm behind his head, eyes closing. "And will someone bring me a croissant with the coffee? I'm starving."

"Lazy people don't get to make demands," Emil snaps as he and Tobias walk toward a small archway tucked in next to the left staircase.

My arm starts to shake from holding the briefcase aloft, and I drop it back to my side with an annoyed huff. "Umm, hello. I have a deal to make?"

"Adie, you sweet mess," Kellen extends an arm to me, fingers curled in invitation. "Come lay on top of me."

My hand tightens around my briefcase as irritation turns to anger. "I'm here for a serious discussion, not to play games."

Kellen bats his lightning-blue eyes at me, his lips formed into a pout. "But I'm cold."

"Then put on some fucking clothes!" I spin on one dirty, bare heel and storm after Tobias and Emil, determined to get this issue settled.

They've stalked me for two days demanding I sign their contract. How dare they disregard me now that I've come to them. A clock ticks in the back of my mind, every second wasted risks the entire contents of my apartment being auctioned off. All because of that lazy ass, sexy demon on the couch.

He should feel lucky I'm ignoring his invitation right now. With the mood I'm in, he's more likely to get a knee to the groin than a cuddle.

I pass through the archway and freeze, eyes wide as I take in the kitchen. Three times the size of the one at my apartment, it fills half of the new room with a large dining table taking up the other half. Dark wood, floor to ceiling cabinets, surround a full-size fridge and freezer on one wall.

At the back, directly across from me, a long, marble counter glows gently, its white surface transformed to a faint pink by the rising sun that comes through a large window. A farm style sink sits beneath it, large enough to fit my full-size baker sheets without problem. An industrial chrome hood hangs over an enormous island in the center of the room, with a six-burner gas stove beneath.

Gaze glued to the island, I drift closer to circle around it. On the other side, I discover side-by-side full-size convection ovens, their glass fronts pristine.

I run my fingertips along the knob controls at the front of the stovetop. With a setup like this, I could bake so many treats.

"Huh. I would have thought that expression was reserved for sex."

Heat floods my cheeks as Tobias's quiet words snap me out of my love affair with their kitchen.

I narrow my eyes on him. "You haven't gotten close to seeing what expression I make during sex."

One eyebrow arches as he takes a sip from his coffee cup. "Pretty sure I did."

I walk down the island until I stand across from them, gaze focused on Kellen. "Bathrooms in coffee shops don't count."

He leans forward on his elbows, the cardboard cup dangling from his fingertips. "The place doesn't matter as long as you're feeling good."

I lean forward, too, until only a foot of counter separates us. "Sucking down your energy has nothing to do with feeling good." The sweet scent of coffee comes from him, and my stomach growls. "I get the same excitement from eating chocolate cake."

"Liar." His eyes drop to my mouth. "You were three seconds away from ripping my pants open."

"You need to control that over inflated ego of yours." His fingers tighten around the coffee cup until the lid pops off and the heat of volcanoes fills the space between us.

His voice rumbles like earthquakes. "Care to put my ego to the test?"

"Yes." I slam my briefcase onto the counter, refusing to show a hint of fear. "That's exactly why I'm here."

"Tobias." Emil's soft voice cuts through the tension and my focus snaps to him.

The ice demon sits on a stool beside his friend, legs crossed and back straight. His coffee cup sits beside him on the counter, a pink bendy straw poking out of the top. The incongruity of this stuffy man sipping his coffee through the pink piece of plastic knocks the fight right out of me. If only I'd had this image three days ago when I met with them at K & B Financial. Maybe then I wouldn't have fled so quickly.

Though I'd needed the time to regroup and come up with an action plan.

Kellen wanders into the kitchen a moment later, scratching his bare abs. "What's all the fuss?"

Emil tips his head toward us. "Adeline and Tobias were performing some kind of combative mating ritual."

I rear back. "We were not!"

"Aww, and I missed it?" Kellen shuffles to the counter and opens a cupboard to pull out a pink box. Lifting the lid, he pulls out a large, buttery croissant. The pastry flakes as he takes a large bite then glances around. "Anyone else want one?"

Emil nods. "On a plate, if you please."

"I'm good with just coffee." Tobias casually straightens, as if he hadn't been close to leaping across the counter, and settles the lid back on his cup.

Kellen turns to me. "Are you hungry, Adie?"

I shiver at the words, almost an exact replica of what Emil said to me not even twenty-four hours ago. Like then, this feels like a trap. I have nothing to trade, though I did bring them coffee, which they already accepted. But that can be seen as part of the negotiation. And since they all accepted the coffees, that means I currently have the favor. If I take the pastry, I lose that slight lead.

I fold my hands over my briefcase. "No, thank you."

"Suit yourself." He fetches a small plate, throws a croissant onto it, then slides it down the counter to Emil, who catches it before it can slide off the edge. Balancing a second pastry on top of his own cup of coffee, Kellen joins the other two men on a stool across from me.

"So, you've come to offer a deal?" Emil prompts once everyone settles. He checks a large watch on his wrist. "You have fifteen minutes."

"Done." I snap the briefcase locks open and pull out a thin stack of paper, sliding it across to Tobias.

He sets his cup aside to flip through the pages. "What's this?"

I meet his questioning gaze. "It's a standard roommate agreement."

He tosses the papers aside. "Why would we want that?"

I square my shoulders and glance at each of them in turn. "Because you are three demons of destruction, desperate to stay on the mortal plane and in need of a succubus roommate. I've already drained off some of your energy over the last few days, but it's only a matter a time before you're back at cataclysmic levels."

If my knowledge of their origin surprises them, they're good at hiding it.

Emil lifts a white eyebrow, his expression bored. "Which is why we offered you the initial contract."

"What you offered me was enslavement, no matter how pretty the terms." I point to the contract in front of Tobias. "What I'm offering is a civil agreement between adults to share a living space."

Kellen takes a bite of croissant and speaks around his mouthful. "That doesn't work for us. We need guarantees that you'll drain our energies on a regular basis."

"Which brings me to the next part of the deal." I pull out another stack of papers, this one larger. "You will absolve me of any backlash from skimming your energies while we are together." I place this part of the contract on top of the roommate agreement. "I will, of course, agree to not take enough to damage your corporeal forms."

My gaze shifts to Emil, who so recently risked his current body yesterday when he gave me free rein to feed off him. He meets my eyes, steady and unrepentant.

Tobias skims through the papers, then passes them to Emil, who takes longer to read them. When Kellen walks over to take a look himself, I shift on my feet, toes numb from the cold tiles of the kitchen floor. The clock on the wall steadily ticks, every minute building toward the auction block.

I clear my throat. "The third part of my deal is with Kellen exclusively."

The storm demon straightens with a broad smile. "Lucky me."

I withdraw a single piece of paper, my signature already on the bottom, and hold it out to him. "Before I will sign any of these documents, you will settle your claim against me."

He folds his arms across his chest and refuses to accept the form. "And why would I do that? You stole from me. These other deals have nothing to do with the actions you took against the humans in my club. That's protected ground, which you violated."

Damn, I'd hoped he would just give in since they

were getting everything they wanted in the first place, just with fewer shackles imposed on me. But I'd planned for the worst and stopped back by Landon's house, where I kept an emergency kit. My mentor hadn't found it yet since that would involve him actually cleaning, something he refuses to do for himself.

When I slip a hand into the front of my shirt, fingers sliding beneath the neon blue cup of my bra, Kellen's eyes widen with anticipation. Does he really only have one thing on his mind?

Shaking my head, I withdraw a tiny vial and set it on the counter in front of him. "This is more than sufficient to cover the energy I stole."

Tobias straightens with sudden, sharp interest, his eyes tracking Kellen's movements as the other man lifts the vial and shakes the glass container. Inside, a drop of iridescent liquid rolls around, tiny rainbows splashing into smaller drops before drawing back together to form a single ball.

Kellen licks his lips, fingers curling protectively around the vial. "Is it one of yours?"

I drop my hands behind the counter so they can't see my clenched fists. "Does it matter?"

Succubus tears are difficult to come by and worth a small fortune on the black market. A feather would have cost me less, but all the ones I've collected over the years are locked up in my apartment. Whether or not it's mine, though, shouldn't matter to anyone except a collector.

I peek at Tobias and shiver. The first time we met, I feared he was a collector of some kind, and the avid interest in his eyes only compounds that concern.

Will I be safe living here?

"I suppose not." Kellen tucks the vial into the waistband of his boxer briefs and gives me a roguish smile. "Though, I'd like to see you cry."

The tension eases from my shoulders. "Pervert."

"Of course." He extends a hand. "Did you bring a pen?"

I fumble in my rush to hand it over, but Kellen catches it smoothly before the sharp tip breaks against the counter.

He taps it against the form, then sets the pen down. "Why should I sign this before you sign the other contracts? What's to stop you from bolting as soon as you're free of the claim against you?"

I lift my chin. "My word."

Emil scoffs, and Tobias snickers. Yeah, I didn't think that would work either.

"What's to stop you from selling off my stuff just

for fun?" At his affronted expression, I add, "I already gave you the tear as a show of trust."

"That was a bad move on your part," Emil points out. "Another sign of how ill-suited you are to business."

I whip around to stare at him, and he jerks his head away from his pink bendy straw. A bead of coffee freezes on his lower lip, and he licks it away before straightening the cardboard insulation sleeve, as if I didn't just catch him in the act. A little of the color fades from his eyes as his stare dares me to comment.

My eyes narrow. "Aren't you just a ray of sunshine today?"

"It can't be helped when a rude person barges into my home at dawn." He checks his watch once more. "Your time is up."

"Look, you cantankerous, stuffed shirt—"

"How dare you—"

"How dare I?" I rise on my tiptoes, my wings an angry vibration along my spine. "If you would pull the icicle out of your—"

"Whoa, there." Kellen shoves half a croissant into my mouth, effectively cutting off my words. He nudges my chin and mimes chewing. "Now isn't that better than fighting?"

Tobias takes the two contracts I handed him and stacks them neatly. "We will agree to these terms provided you move in today."

I choke down the pastry and croak out a protest, "But I haven't even packed."

"Already taken care of." With a sigh, Kellen lifts the pen once more.

He presses the needle-sharp tip into the meat of his index finger to draw a drop of blood, then scrawls his name across the bottom of his form, relinquishing his claim against me. With both of our signatures in place, the paper vanishes. It should arrive at the Clerk's Office within the hour, well before my apartment goes up for auction.

I stare at the empty counter top, a weight lifting from my shoulders now that my possessions are safe. Then his words sink in and my head snaps up. "What do you mean it's already taken care of?"

He shrugs as he passes the pen to Tobias. "Everything had to be boxed up for sale anyway, so I had it brought here."

"Th—that's—" The rage that spikes through me makes it impossible for me to form sentences. How dare they touch my things? What if I'd been able to dispute his claim?

"That's convenient," Tobias supplies as he signs both contracts. "You should thank us."

"There is, of course, the small cost of paying the movers." Emil doesn't glance up, intent on neatly signing his name on the next line.

"Movers?" I rub my hand over my hair, my fingers tangling in the matted locks.

Kellen bounces over to sign his own name, then shoves the pen and contracts back across the island to me. They butt up against my briefcase, the names still glistening wetly.

"Yes, movers." Tobias says slowly. "How else were you planning to get your stuff here?"

"In my car?" My meager bank account can't afford professionals, especially not after all the gas and fast food of the last few days.

"I've seen your car. It never would have fit." Emil sniffs and slides off his stool. "I'm going back to bed for an hour. Don't disturb me."

"Yes, Mr. Fussy Pants," I mutter under my breath.

His steps hesitate for a moment, but he strides from the room without glancing back. A moment later the stairs creak as he goes back to his bedroom.

Helpless, I stare at Tobias and Kellen, feeling like I got caught in my own trap. "I can't afford to pay the movers."

"That's okay, we'll just tack it onto your rent." Kellen stretches, the muscles on his chest rippling. "I'll be back up at noon if you need help unpacking."

And what would that cost me? "I think I'll manage on my own, but thank you."

"Suit yourself." With a wave, he shuffles out of the kitchen.

Left alone with Tobias, I lift the pen and sign my name beneath theirs, sealing my fate. When I finish, I pass them back to him and beg, "Please show me to your nearest shower."

(UN)HAPPY

I triple check the lock on the bathroom door while the water heats up in the shower. In an old house like this, with the water heater in the basement, the hot water has a long way to travel.

When Tobias walked me upstairs and showed me the bathroom, I'd been surprised to find it so small. After the kitchen, I expected a grand, five-piece bath. Instead, I walked into a room the size of a closet. The door bangs against the claw-footed tub when open, and the pedestal sink with zero excess counter space barely fits next to the short toilet.

But it smells of lemons and soap, and the white, octagon-tiled floor sparkles with a fresh cleaning. No toothpaste marks the sink, and the wastebasket, neatly tucked between the sink and the wall, doesn't even hold a ball of tissue inside.

Nice and clean.

At least, it was until I left dirty footsteps all over it.

I shrug and finish brushing my teeth. Once I'm out of the shower, I can wipe up the footprints with my used towel. Behind me, steam rolls out of the shower, and I eagerly drop my toothbrush into the holder beside a bright-blue one, strip out of my filthy clothes, and hop over the high side of the tub, whisking the shower curtain closed.

As soon as I find my bubble bath, I plan to take a long bath. But for now, I turn the knob to send the water up into the retro-fitted shower head that hangs from the ceiling. A hot waterfall rushes over my head.

So decadent.

Briefly, I wonder how big the heater is since a shower like this must drain it fast, but then I shrug. It wouldn't be here if it didn't last at least ten minutes, right?

With a sigh of relief, I let my wings slip from my back and rustle the feathers beneath the spray. It feels good to let them stretch for the first time since my hurried shower the morning of my ill-fated meeting with the bank.

The shampoo left in the shower has that odd smell that all scent-free products seem to give off. Glad it's not *musk of man* or whatever those cologne heavy soaps call themselves, I lather up and soap down my entire body, happy beyond belief to wash the dirt, stick, and who knows what else down the drain.

Then, I lean back my head and enjoy the shower's warmth, letting the slow transition toward lukewarm let me know when it's time to get out.

I jerk back to awareness when the bathroom door rattles, wings fleeing back to safety within my body. The door crashes open with a loud bang against the tub, vibrating the cast iron beneath my feet.

A moment later, the curtain pulls back with a loud rattle, and Emil scowls in at me. "You better not have used up all the hot water."

My hands go to my hips. "A little privacy, please?"

"I have an actual job to go to, you know." He sticks an arm under the spray, and his scowl deepens. "You used up the entire tank?"

Quickly, I shut off the water and grab a towel, wrapping it around myself. As I wind a smaller one around my hair, I demand, "Aren't you supposed to be sleeping?"

"You've been in here for an hour." As if only just now registering my nudity, his gaze rakes over me. "Do you have no concept of time?"

My wings rustle with agitation. I don't like the

disadvantage of my position, trapped within the tub. But there's not enough space in the bathroom to get out without Emil moving.

At least the tub gives me a few inches in height so I can glare directly into his eyes. "I'm sorry, I was enjoying the first shower I've had in days."

He leans closer, his sleep-tousled, white hair falling across his forehead. "It's not my fault you're not self-sufficient enough to figure out a way to stay clean."

I stiffen with affront. "I was homeless!"

The blue slowly fades from his eyes, the temperature in the room dropping. "You seemed cozy enough at that incubus's house."

My bones rattle with warning, but I refuse to be cowed. "Someone chased me out first thing in the morning."

One side of his mouth quirks up. "I seem to remember you running away."

"That's called a tactical retreat."

"You dented my car." His eyes fade to complete white. "You dirtied my clean bathroom." The beads of water on my skin turn to crystals of ice. "Now, you stole my hot water."

I lick my lips, tasting the energy that fills the small room. Fresh snow, metallic and clean. This demon can bring on a new ice age. He should terrify me—and he does to some degree—but if we're going to be roommates, I can't let him push me around.

Closing the small distance between us, I press our noses together, heedless of the nip of frost against my skin. "I'll clean the bathroom and make you some hot chocolate for when you're done with your lukewarm shower. Sound good?"

If anything, the temperature drops further. "Are you trying to appease me?"

"It's a peace offering." I blow warm air across his lips, and he rears back, his brows furrowed in confusion.

He sniffs and backs against the wall to give me room to climb out of the tub. "Why would you think we'd have hot chocolate here?"

"Just a hunch." My eyes drop to the tiled floor as I step onto the small bath mat. My footprints are all over the place. With a sigh, I tug the towel from my hair and drop it, using my foot on top of it to wipe up the mess.

When I gather it and my dirty clothes up, I turn to glance at Emil, brows raised in question.

His eyes, back to their regular shade of blue, study me before he nods. "The packets are in the top left drawer of the kitchen island."

"And the straws?" After thinking about it for a minute earlier, I'd figured out he used one with his coffee to avoid touching the actual cup with his icy lips, prolonging the warmth inside a little longer.

For a moment, I think he'll try to pretend he doesn't know what I'm talking about, but then he glances away. "They're in a dispenser on the counter next to the fridge."

"Excellent." I step closer to him to make enough room to open the door. "See? We can be civil to each other."

His lips tighten. "I've always been civil."

"I'm going to buy you a dictionary." With another puff of warm air in his face, I zip out of the bathroom, slamming the door behind.

Back in the kitchen, I turn the burner on under the tea kettle that waits on top of the stove. It clicks for a moment, then blue flames burst from beneath the kettle. My knees shake with excitement as the gas comes to life, and I spend an embarrassingly long time stroking the stainless steel beauty while the water boils.

Adjusting the towel, I crouch to investigate the

large oven. Instead of a regular pull down door, this one features French doors that open to either side, allowing for easier access. Three full-sized racks, evenly spaced, fill the interior, and the bottom of the oven shines, no hint of soot in sight. Do they ever cook for themselves?

"Don't worry," I coo to the pristine interior. "I'm here now, and I'm going to bake so many yummy desserts in you."

"What are you doing?"

I spring to my feet to find Tobias on the other side of the island from me. He had changed into a business suit, similar to the one he wore the last time I saw him at the bank, only with faint, dark-gray pinstripes.

His black eyes rake over me, and his mouth kicks up into an amused smile. "The towel's an interesting choice, but I prefer naked apron play."

Resisting the urge to clutch the knot at my front to make sure the thin piece of terry cloth stays in place, I scowl at him. "I don't do naked apron play."

He arches an eyebrow in disbelief. "No?"

Heat creeps across my shoulders and chest as I recall the one time while I still lived in Dreamland when I did, in fact, play housewife, wearing only an apron. But Dreamland and the human plane are different. People dream about a lot of things, and as a succubus, it's my job to make sure they're the happiest they can be so they release the most energy.

On the human plane, though, building elaborate fantasies takes more energy than I can safely gain, so I need to take more from the humans. Also, humans on the physical plane have a lot less stamina than their dream selves, which means I barely start to feed before they're finished.

Skimming is easier all around, even if it takes more time.

The tea kettle's whistle saves me from having to answer Tobias's question. Quickly, I move it off the burner, then pull open the drawer in the island where Emil said I would find what I need.

Holy hot chocolate heaven.

Fancy metallic packets of powder, from white chocolate to dark chocolate with flavor options including caramel, mint, raspberry, and cinnamon, line the drawer.

I lift one out and flip it over to read the directions, then peek at Tobias, who circled around the counter while I was distracted. "Do all of these require hot milk?"

"Yep." He steps closer to open the drawer next to mine and pulls out a packet of green tea, then he nudges the lower cabinet with the toe of his shiny black loafer. "The saucepan is down there. Don't scald the milk."

"I know how to heat milk." Grumbling, I bend to find the small sauce pan with a pour lip on one side.

Spotting it near the back, I reach for it and feel a slight tug on my towel. The stupid knot at the front unravels in an instant, and I drop the pan to yank the material closed.

Re-knotting it, I grab the pan's handle and straighten to poke it against Tobais's rock hard stomach. "Stop that."

He pushes the pan aside, unrepentant. "Do you often walk around in a towel at home? A robe would be better. Something in silk, maybe?"

Like I own anything that fancy. "I have to find my clothes before I can get dressed."

On the way to the bathroom earlier, Tobias had pointed out the stairs that led up to my new room. When I'd ventured up to get dressed, I found boxes stacked haphazardly around my furniture, the small couch from my old living room leaning against the bed, with no sign of a suitcase in sight. My dirty clothes and towel sit in a neat stack on one edge of the counter, which reminds me…

I glance at Tobias. “Where’s the washing machine?”

“I think there’s one in the basement.” He shrugs and turns away to get a mug from the cupboard next to the refrigerator.

“You think?” I follow behind him to fetch the milk. “You don’t know?”

“We have a service that comes on Sundays to clean the house and take our laundry to the dry cleaners.”

“Lucky you.” Rich bastards. I open the fridge, unsurprised when I discover it stocked mostly with bottled water, wine, milk, and one lone, wrinkly apple. Grocery shopping just moved up on my list. “Do you have food delivered, too?”

“We mostly eat out, though Kellen usually picks up a box of pastries on his way home from the club in the morning.”

I walk back to the stove and pour the milk into the pan before turning the stove on low. “Is food and laundry included in the rent?”

He laughs at my hopeful tone. “Did you include it in the contract we signed?”

My shoulders hunch. It never even crossed my mind that that was an option.

He tugs a strand of my damp hair, rubbing the

fine blue tips between his fingers. "Do you want to renegotiate?"

"No need." I swat him away. "I'm perfectly capable of doing those things myself."

"If you say so."

I bristle at his obvious doubt. "Look, I realize I might have come across as a little desperate the first time we met—"

"A little?"

Ignoring him, I forge on, "But I've been taking care of myself just fine. If I hadn't run into you on accident at the coffee shop, I'd be well into the launch phase of my bakery right now."

He studies me for a moment, face serious. "You know, our paths were bound to cross, no matter what."

"What are you talking about?" I bump him aside and randomly select a hot chocolate mix from the drawer. "If I hadn't given into my cousin's offer to use HelloHell Delivery, none of this would have happened."

He shakes his head. "You're exactly where you were always going to be."

I scoff, "That's stupid."

"You're naive." When I bristle, he holds up a

hand. "If we hadn't met at the coffee shop, what would have happened?"

"I'd have peacefully gotten my loan and been happily hunting for a shop location right now." Grumbling, I stir the milk on the stovetop as small bubbles begin to appear.

Tobias leans a hip against the counter while he waits for his tea to steep. "And how would you have prepared for your meeting at the bank?"

The spoon slows to a stop as I peek at him from the corner of my eye. "I would have gone to the club to fill up on energy."

He gives a knowing nod, the smug bastard. "Where you would have met Kellen."

"And if I hadn't gone to the club…" I push out an annoyed breath. "Let me guess. Emil reviews all demon loan applications. So I would have met both of you at the bank, where you would have refused my loan anyway."

"Ding, ding, ding." Tobias pulls the tea bag from his mug and tosses it into the trash before giving me a sympathetic pat on the shoulder. "Like I said, you were always going to end up here."

I shrug his hand off, then grab a to-go mug I noticed in the cupboard and add the hot chocolate mix to it before carefully pouring in the hot milk.

When I glance up at him, he looks entirely too satisfied. "You know, I could have decided to leave town."

He smiles over the rim of his mug. "You're far too stubborn for that."

"So what's your point?" I screw the cap on tight and shake the container, taking my annoyance out on the cocoa.

"Stop mourning the loss of your shop because it was never meant to happen. Just embrace your new position as our household succubus."

I slam the mug down on the counter and whip around to face him. "What is with you guys and being assholes? Are you so old and crotchety that you've forgotten what basic manners are?"

"Crotchety?" The way he draws out the word makes it sound like he's never heard it before.

"*Old* and crotchety." I jab my finger against his chest. "Maybe you've had centuries to amass your fortune and dig out a place in the human world that you fit into nicely, but some of us lowly demons are still struggling here. So get your jollies pissing on my dreams all you want, but I am telling you here and now that I am *no one's* kept succubus. I'm your roommate who has the *option* to help you out with your energy issues. Because don't think for a second that anywhere in those contracts you signed did it say I *had* to feed off you." I step back and gesture to my body. "This right here? Not for your use."

His eyes narrow as he stalks forward. "Is that a threat? You're not living here if you're not useful to us."

"It's a statement of fact." My bones rattle with imminent danger, and I force myself to hold my ground as the air fills with the metallic taste of thunderstorms. Meeting his black eyes, I lift my chin. "You may be powerful and able to destroy entire cities in one night, but that means you need me more than I need you."

He leans over me, a rolling cloud of thunder. "We can get a different succubus."

"Then do it." I put my hands on my hips to hide their tremble. "I'll even give you a list of names."

His nostrils flare as he drags my scent into his lungs. "You're a weak little succubus who can't even take care of herself."

I rise up onto my toes. "And you're a big, bad catalyst demon who's scared of losing his corporeal form."

Lightning skates over my skin, and I lock my knees, unwilling to back down even if it means being obliterated by his wrath.

"Tobias," Emil's calm voice breaks through the tension, "We need to leave for work."

I drop back to my heels, then skirt around the angry demon to grab the to-go mug off the counter. I thrust it into Emil's hand on my way out of the kitchen and head for the curved staircase that leads up to my new room.

Emil's voice drifts after me. "Call the bank to set up a new appointment. I think I've just reconsidered your loan."

I pause, one foot on the wooden step, to glance back over my shoulder. Emil stands in the archway, mug raised as if to salute me. With a nod, I walk calmly up the steps.

I'm not sure if that was a victory or not, but I'll take it.

Grade A Something

"Darling, I'm so glad to hear you resolved that pesky little issue you were having," Julian's happy voice fills the phone. "And the cousins are having a proper cat fight over that old apartment of yours. I think I'll be able to raise the rent by a couple hundred."

"You could have given me a little heads up." I pull another pillow over my body, wiggling to ensconce myself beneath the pile. It doesn't feel the same as my old home. The bed faces the wrong way, the large room giving sounds a different echo.

"I knew you could figure it out on your own." A creak sounds, and I picture Julian kicking his feet up in his office at HelloHell Delivery. "You're resilient when backed into a corner."

"Speaking of corners, how'd you do against cousin Cassandra?" I tuck a pillow against my stomach, the blue feathers stabbing me through the tank top I pulled on earlier. I hadn't found my favorite pillow with the purple sequins. This one doesn't fit quite right, the size a little too small, the stuffing too flat.

"Oh, were you worried for me?" Humor fills his tone.

I actually was, which is the main reason I called. I knew he would have already heard about the claim against me being reversed. Julian's delivery demons bring him all the best gossip. "Did she eat your mischief imp?"

"Only a small nibble. Poor thing will recover." He sounds nonchalant, but a hint of weariness underscores his words.

Of all of my kind, Cousin Cassandra scares me the most. She's one of the oldest of our kind, filled with energies gathered over almost a millennia of life. Everyone is open game, even her own kind. And not in the distracted, lazy way that my mentor, Landon, skims my energy. Cassandra is an active, frequently malicious, devourer.

My voice drops to a whisper. "And you?"

He stays quiet long enough that I think he won't answer, but then his gruff voice mumbles, "I'll be fine, darling."

"I'm sorry if I was the reason she came to visit." I

curl tighter around the too small pillow, the pointy feathers little stabs of recrimination.

"Hush. She would have stopped by anyway. You were just an added treat." He clears his throat. "Speaking of treats, I heard you're now living with some grade A energy."

"They're grade A something," I grumble and wiggle until my back presses against the headboard.

His voice brightens. "Oh, trouble in paradise already?"

I snort, still annoyed by my exchange with Tobias. "We're still feeling each other out."

"Oh, that sounds delicious. Tell me more."

I huff in exasperation. "Not like that."

"No, of course not." Julian sounds equally exasperated. "I blame Landon for your failings as a succubus. He was far too young and lazy to raise you right."

My wings shiver against my spine, instantly defensive. "He did his best."

"You're sweet, darling, but no he didn't." The creak comes again, followed by a thump. "I'm going to the club tonight. Should I pop by your new place to pick you up?"

"You're not getting an invitation to come investigate that easily."

"You rude child. I was only thinking about you."

"No, you were only thinking about laying your eyes on my new roommates."

"More than my eyes," he purrs. "The rumors I've heard…"

I perk up in an instant. The way he trails off, means he has some juicy gossip, but he won't give it away for free. I try to sound disinterested. "Oh?"

His tone turns sly. "Invite me over, and I'll tell you all about them."

A gentle knock on the doorframe pulls me from the pile of pillows. Over the fluffy mound, I spot Kellen lounging in the open doorway. He put on more clothes this time, a soft pair of flannel lounge pants and a t-shirt that hugs his muscular chest.

I lift the phone to my ear once more. "I'll talk to you later."

"But what abou—"

His voice cuts off as I hit the end button and set the phone aside. Petting the blue pillow in my arms, I smooth down the decorative feathers as I stare at Kellen. "Are you here to be mean to me, too?"

"Someone sounds like they need a hug." He straightens and takes a step into the room.

"Stop!" I point at him, and he freezes, one foot

still in the air. "This is my room. I didn't invite you inside."

"Ahh." He takes an exaggerated step back and resumes his position in the doorway. "Had a bad morning?"

"Your friends are assholes." I abandon the pillow and crawl to the opposite end of the bed to see him better. "You're an asshole, too. I'm living with a group of assholes."

He winces. "We're not that bad."

I flop onto my back to stare at the high ceiling. Open rafters crisscross the high peak. They put me at the top of the east facing tower in what can loosely be termed a finished attic space. "I have yet to see compelling evidence to the contrary."

Since he can't argue, he ignores my statement. "Do you want help unpacking?"

I fold my arms over my stomach. "Didn't you already paw through my stuff enough?"

"Well, actually, I wasn't there to oversee the movers." A board creaks as he shifts his weight. "Your cousin let them in."

"Figures." I snort, unsurprised by Julian's betrayal. As he'd said before, he had his own interests to look after first. Demons, as a whole, are selfish creatures. Head turning, I see Kellen settled cross-legged on the floor outside my doorway. "One of my pillows is missing."

He leans to one side to take a long look at the large pile at my headboard. "How can you tell?"

"They're mine. I know." I sniff and return my attention to the ceiling. Overhead, the crisscrossing beams form a pentagram. Fantastic. "It's a purple sequined, square pillow, one and a half feet square."

"It might still be in one of the boxes," he offers, sounding uninterested.

Annoyance skitters through me. He would care if it were something of his that went missing. "I looked. It's not."

Despite the apparent disarray, I already sorted through the boxes and separated them into kitchen, bedroom, bathroom, and living room. But that doesn't mean I have anywhere to put those items. I need to investigate the kitchen to see what I have double of, and the bathroom I apparently share with Emil doesn't offer a lot of space for my stuff.

I picture the fussy demon's face if he came back to discover a new shower caddy and shelves to hold my products. Maybe a floor cart. He'd probably blow a gasket. I curl my legs up to my stomach to hug my knees, ridiculously happy at the idea.

Kellen's voice interrupts my imagining. "How do you like the room?"

"There's no closet." I discovered that right away, so even after a quick hunt located my suitcases, they remain packed.

At my apartment, I didn't need a dresser. It's really the only thing I can come up with to complain about. The room offers more than enough space to put my bedroom set and living room furniture in and still have excess floor space for new furniture. Aside from needing the bathroom and kitchen, I could make this my own little apartment and never have to interact with the others.

I frown at the thought.

Is that why they gave me such a big room? Am I expected to stay out of their way unless they need me to drain their energy? My focus shifts to my small, floral printed couch. I'm dragging it downstairs the first chance I get.

Prepare to be invaded, bachelor pad.

"There might be a dresser in the basement." Kellen's voice pulls my narrowed, suspicious gaze his way, and he shrugs. "The last succubus left all her stuff here, so we just had it moved downstairs. She was a huge headache like that." When I don't immediately leap up, he adds, "It's all unclaimed goods."

"Oh?" I sit up, interested despite myself. Unclaimed goods mean I won't have to offer anything in trade for them. If there really is furniture available, it will save my poor bank account from total destitution.

He rises smoothly to his feet with a smile. "And to show I'm not a complete asshole, I'll even help carry up whatever you want."

I bounce off the bed and shove my feet into my sneakers. "So you admit you're somewhat of an asshole?"

His smile broadens into a grin. "I'm a demon."

"That's a weak excuse." Chin up, I march past him and down the stairs.

On the second floor landing, we bypass the bathroom and a closed door that I assume hides Emil's room. When I paused next to it earlier, the air outside smelled like him. Did they put him up here so any icy power surges he has won't interfere with them?

I glance over my shoulder. "Do you and Tobias have rooms in the west tower?"

"Yep. Tobias has the middle floor, and I have the top, like you." As we reach the ground floor, he points to the curved staircase on the right side of the fireplace before batting his eyelashes at me. "If we both open our shutters, we can see into each other's towers." His eyebrows waggle. "I walk around in the nude, in case you're interested."

I widen my eyes at him in mock fascination. "Is this a scheduled event? Should I bring popcorn?"

He nods solemnly. "We can string two soup cans together so I can call and let you know when the show starts."

I can't hold back the snort of laughter. "I look forward to it."

"Ah, there it is!" He points at my face. "I knew there was a smile in there somewhere."

I scowl up at him. "I'm actually a very happy person."

"And now it's gone." His fingers drift down my bare arm, leaving a path of lightning sparks behind, before he laces our fingers together. "Come on. The basement's this way."

He tugs me toward the kitchen.

Without a conscious effort to resist them, the tiny pricks seep through my skin and into my belly. I shiver despite myself. Unused to such frequent doses of energy, I can't stop myself from shifting closer until I walk alongside him, my arm pressing against his.

The place where our skin meets tingles, a buzz of warmth that suffuses my whole body in a light flush.

If Kellen notices, he doesn't comment as we enter the kitchen and he leads me to a door on the right, tucked in next to the dining table, that I'd assumed led to a pantry.

When he pulls it open, a flickering, overhead light comes on to reveal a narrow, wooden staircase. One of those types with an open back that anyone can reach through to grab the person walking down them. They remind me of every horror movie I've ever seen where the blond girl gets murdered by the psycho who lives in the basement.

My fingers tighten in reflex, crushing Kellen's hand before I force myself to release him and step forward. Time to be a brave little succubus. Or a stupidly dead one.

Bargain Shopping

He crowds against my back in a rush of sparks. "Use the handrail. The steps aren't evenly spaced."

I discover that for myself a moment later when my heel slams into the third step down, finding resistance way before I expected to. Stumbling, I grab the thin rail mounted to the stairs as Kellen fists the back of my tank top to steady me.

"Whoa, there." His chest presses against my back, hand sliding to cup my ribcage. "You okay?"

I study the steep flight of stairs and give the railing an experimental tug. It wobbles, the wall brackets loose. "These stairs can't be legal."

Back still pressed against him, I feel his chest move as he shrugs. "There weren't any building codes back when the house was built."

"Why haven't you fixed it?" Cautious now, I

locate the next step with the toe of my sneaker before putting my weight down on it. Carrying furniture back up will be dangerous.

"No reason to when we don't come down here often."

As we pass below the line of the floor above, the wall disappears to reveal a large room, stuffed haphazardly with furniture and boxes. Against the left wall, I locate what looks to be an ancient washer and dryer, buried in the mess. My shoulders sag. It will take forever to dig a path to reach them.

My gaze sweeps over the room. "All of this can't be from the last succubus."

"Our furniture from the last two remodels is down here, too." His breath ruffles the hair over my ear as he whispers loudly. "Emil is a bit of a hoarder."

"Seriously?" A couple sheet draped pieces look like couches, and I spot a giant tube television. "It's a waste of space."

"As long as it doesn't impact the upper floors, we don't really care."

"Yeah," I agree. "The clutter probably wouldn't make Emil happy."

"Oh, you picked up on that already?" Kellen sounds surprised.

"He's a clean freak, right?" Emil's annoyance at

the mess I made in the bathroom gave him away. Even if they have a cleaner in once a week, the pristine sink and trash can scream fussiness.

"He likes things to be in their place," Kellen says noncommittally.

When we reach the bottom of the stairs, I pause, unsure where to start. The amount of stuff down here is daunting.

"Oh, look, there's a dresser." He announces and circles around me to lift a piece of furniture from the cement floor.

Envy rushes through me at the easy show of strength as he settles the large dresser back on its feet. I'd have to drain precious energy to do the same. The upper level demons sure have it easy.

We don't get to choose the shape our corporeal forms take when we come to the human plane. While in Dreamland, I'd gotten used to looking like a model, the centerfold of young male fantasies. Statuesque, with lean muscles. I'd been less than pleased to be handed an average height, physically weak body when I finally figured out how to escape Dreamland. While still stronger than humans, and worlds above imps, succubus land squarely in the middle ground of the demon pecking order.

Kellen brushes dust off the top of the dresser as I

come closer. The clean, solid lines and seven drawers would work perfectly for me. I tug on one chrome knob to pull the center drawer open. It glides smoothly, as do the rest of the drawers when I test them.

"Well, that was easy." I give one side an experimental lift and groan as it only makes it an inch off the floor. "I'm not going to be a lot of help getting it up the stairs, though."

Kellen props an elbow up on the top, and it thunks back down. "Oh, this isn't one of the unclaimed pieces."

I glance from him to the dresser. "What?"

"This one is mine." He points over my shoulder. "The unclaimed items are over there."

Following his direction, I find a sheet draped pile on the other side of the stairs. When I whisk away the cover, I stumble back in horror. "You can't be serious."

Kellen comes up behind me, amusement in his voice. "I told you she was a headache."

I stare, open mouthed, at the fuchsia-colored furniture. The dresser and nightstand bubble out at the sides and the spindly legs point inward and end on narrow spikes. Swirls of gold outline the frame, and crystal drawer pulls catch the flickering overhead lights and cast rainbow sparkles across the floor. They look like they came from a cartoon. A horrible cartoon created by people on drugs.

When I cautiously approach the dresser to pull out one of the narrow drawers, the entire thing tips forward, too lightweight and the narrow legs too close together to offer proper support.

Turning, I peek back at the first dresser. Sleek lines, sturdy construction, solid wood.

Kellen ducks into my line of sight, eyebrow raised. "Do you want to bargain for the other one?"

I meet his lightning blue eyes. "What do you want?"

"What do you have to offer?" He crowds close until sparks skip from his skin to mine, static electricity that makes my hair rise and my yoga pants cling to my legs.

Not for the first time, I notice how his energy calls to me in a way that Tobias's and Emil's don't. While I crave theirs, Kellen's hungers to be inside me. It dives past my stomach, hunting deeper for the ball of light that sits at my core, that life force that makes me a succubus. In all my years, no other energy has ever affected me in this way.

I lick ozone from the air and shiver. "Why does it do that?"

"Do what?" He steps closer, mesmerizing like a storm cloud ready to crash over me.

"This." I wave my hand through the air between us, now thick with power.

At our first encounter, he pulled the energy from me. Something only succubi should be able to do. But when I took it back, it came eagerly, flooding through my body. Most energy resists at first, clinging to the life form it inhabits. But not his.

Lightning streaks across his pupils. "You're made of passion and born in storms. We call to each other."

I back away, unwilling to be overwhelmed by him, and knock against the dresser. It teeters back, ready to fall, and Kellen reaches past me to steady it, his body coming flush with mine. I find my face pressed into his throat, my nose filling with his scent.

My entire front tingles, and he gives a shaky sigh of relief. His cheek rests against the side of my head, his breath warm. "That feels so good."

I remember he'd asked me to lay on top of him earlier. At the time, I thought he'd been asking for sex, but maybe he really did just want me to absorb some of his power.

Nose pressed to his throat, I mumble, "Why do you have so much built up? I drained you three days ago."

"There's a storm coming." One hand curves over my lower back to pull me closer, and the hard bulge of his erection presses against my stomach.

His actions right now don't feel sexual, though, which confuses me. "So the storm's recharging you or something?"

"She's wooing me." His head lifts, and when I glance up, I find his eyes focused on the ceiling, as if he can see through the house to the sky beyond. "She's small, but she wants to be bigger."

Longing fills his voice, a deep, ingrained desire to answer the storm's call. At the demon library, I saw images of the destruction that comes when he gives into the storm's call. Cities wiped out through floods, homes swept up in hurricanes, wildfires spread through lightning.

My plans for the future don't include relocating once again, so I wrap my arms around him, slip my arms beneath his shirt, and draw the power from his body into mine. He shudders within my hold, muscles tensing and relaxing, as if he wants to fight and forces himself to be still.

My wings shiver against my spine with the need to be free, to take to the air and be among the clouds. I hold a tsunami in my arms, and my bones tell me that similar, smaller power sweeps toward the city, a ready supply to glut myself on.

But I know the call of a siren when I hear it. Destruction waits in the sky, a cruel mistress ready to rip me apart to feed herself. I shove the energy into my belly and Emil's power, already there, curls around it, restraining it with an icy swiftness that leaves my legs shaky.

My arms drop to my sides, and Kellen moves away, neither of us willing to acknowledge what just happened.

I clear my throat. "So, I get the other dresser?"

He adjusts his pants, and one corner of his mouth tips up. "I don't remember us agreeing to a price."

"But—"

He taps his chin in thought. "Got any more tears stashed away?"

My hands fly to my hips. "That dresser isn't worth a tear!"

"Well, that really depends on how much you want it." He grins, eyes bright. "It's a seller's market right now."

"I like the pink one just fine," I grumble.

"Aww. Not even going to try to bargain me down?" He *tsks* under his breath. "We need to work on your demon skills."

"My skills are just fine."

"That's debatable."

Annoyed, I step to one side of the ugly dresser. "Get your muscled ass over here and help me carry this horrible thing up to my room."

He straightens, entirely too happy. "You've been looking at my ass?"

I grip the edges and lift experimentally, almost knocking the piece of furniture over. "Hard not to when you walk around in your underwear."

He lifts from his side, taking most of the weight, and stares at me over the top, face serious. "Your ass is nice, too."

"Of course it is. I'm a succubus." I sniff with disdain. "Now shut up, and start walking."

"You want to go up first?" He takes a step to the side, and I stumble to stay on my feet.

I glance at the steep flight, with the uneven steps. No way I want to walk up those backward. "You're buff, you go up first."

"It's easier if the taller person holds the bottom," he points out, voice full of logic.

"You know, this thing is pretty light." I bounce it to demonstrate. "You can probably carry it up on your own."

He purses his lips, thoughtful. "I said I'd help, not do all the work."

"It would be faster without me in the way." I can play the logic card, too.

His head tilts to one side as he studies me. "But, I like to watch you struggle."

"And there's that little bit of asshole."

He grins and nods toward the stairs. "Up you go."

I glance back at the matching nightstands and shudder. Whoever designed this bedroom set needs to be shot. If it were mine, I'd have left it behind, too. Curious about my predecessor, I turn back to Kellen. "I've been meaning to ask. What happened to your last succubus?"

He studies me for a long moment, the creepy overhead lights casting shadows over his face, before he shrugs. "We ate her."

Chainsaws

We ate her, rings in my ears as I drop the dresser and put on speed to get the hell out of the basement.

A loud crack sounds, followed by Kellen's deep belly laugh. I freeze, halfway up the stairs, and turn back to find him leaning against the fuchsia piece of furniture, clutching his sides as he howls with glee.

Face split into a wide grin, he points up at me. "Oh, you should have seen your face!"

"That was a joke?" I zoom down the uneven wooden stairs in a blur to shove his shoulder. "Shut up! That's not funny!"

He stumbles to the side, still laughing, as he bangs his fist against his knee. "We! Ate! Her!"

Arms crossed under my breasts, I glare at him, sneaker-covered foot tapping against the cement floor. "Well, I wouldn't put it past you lot."

With a smirk, he hooks his fingers in front of his face to imitate fangs. "Grr. Argh."

Annoyed I fell for his joke so easily, I turn to study the dresser. One of the spindly legs broke when I dropped it, and it now leans precariously. "You're ridiculous."

"No, you're ridiculous."

"So what really happened to your last succubus?"

As he straightens to stare down at me, the amusement slips from his expression. "She flew the coop as soon as her term ran out."

My brow furrows in confusion. "You didn't have her locked down in some impossible-to-escape contract?"

"No. Up until recently, we only committed to twenty year arrangements." His lips purse. Avoiding my gaze, he focuses on a stack of trunks that rise in a precarious tower to lean against the side of the staircase. "The last one was a headache, but we'd gotten used to her. Settled into our routine. We were going to sign her again, but she skipped out."

I study his face. He doesn't appear sad, but something about the tightness around his mouth makes me question, "Do you miss her?"

He huffs out a laugh. "Not at all. Like I said, she was a headache." Then, his eyes snap to mine. "Emil wanted to hunt her down, though. Make her sign again. He doesn't do well with change."

"Was that Plan B?" I remember Emil muttering something about that when we met at the bank.

Kellen shrugs. "Who knows. Emil has so many contingency plans, I stopped trying to keep track of them."

I file that tidbit of information away for later. "So, how many succubi have you had?"

The tightness returns to his face as he glances away. "Four."

His stiff shoulders let me know I'm pushing against some forbidden subject, but curiosity gets the better of me. "That doesn't seem like enough, with only twenty year contracts. Did the others resign?"

"No." The single word comes out clipped.

These three demons have lived for centuries. They would have needed at least ten succubi by now. Unless they went back to the demon realm for a time. But the library books seemed to imply they'd remained on Earth.

I nibble my lip, considering. "But the Destruction Laws went into effect two-hundred years ago."

When Kellen remains silent, I venture down a new path. "How long have you lived with Tobias and Emil?"

"It's getting late. You want help carrying this lovely monstrosity up, or not?" He puts a hand on the dresser, then catches it as it tips backward.

"It's broken." I crouch to grab the detached leg off the floor and use it to indicate the far more sturdy dresser he originally tempted me with. "You should give me that one as a replacement."

"You're the one who dropped it," he points out. There's that stupid logic again. "Glue it back together."

Opening one of the drawers, I drop the leg inside before reassuming my position. "Okay, let's get this over with."

By the time we make it from the basement to the top of the third story, my thighs burn. I shift my grip on the dresser, sweaty palms making my grip weak, and carry the ugly thing through my doorway.

Kellen drops his end the second it passes into my room, and the legs scratch across the floor. Surprised, I stare at him over the top. "What's wrong?"

"You said I can't enter your room." He purses his lips and leans to the side to see as much of the space as possible. "Are you hiding something fun I should be aware of?"

"Nope."

With a grunt, I lift the dresser and waddle to the left wall where the boxes leave an area wide enough to wedge it in. When it tips sideways, I drag a box over to prop under the broken corner until I can buy some glue.

Kellen leans against the doorframe, arms folded over his chest. "Do you want the matching nightstands?"

"Hell, no." Straightening, I grab one of my suitcases and open it. As I discovered earlier, the movers didn't take the time to fold my clothes and they lay in a wadded, disorganized clump, with the hangers still attached.

Kellen taps his foot in annoyance at being ignored. "Do you want lunch?"

I shake out a blouse, the wrinkles forming deep creases in the delicate material, and set it aside to be ironed. When I glance at him, his foot stills. "Are you lonely? Or are you trying to trick me into taking something that doesn't belong to me so you can demand payment?"

His mouth quirks at one corner. "So suspicious."

I sniff as I pull out a skirt, setting it off to the side. "Tobias already made it clear that food isn't included in my living arrangements."

The amused expression that always seems to be on Kellen's face slips away. "Tobias and Emil really aren't that bad, once you get to know them."

"I'll change my opinion when they give me reason to." Beneath a sweatshirt, I find a small dry erase board.

It came from my kitchen, the remnants of a recipe I'd been playing with now smeared to the point of being illegible. Annoyed, I march to one of the boxes with the food from my pantry and shove it inside.

Lifting the box, I turn to Kellen. "Come on. You can show me which cupboard will be mine."

Confused, he steps out of the way. "Which cupboard?"

"For my stuff." I pass him and walk down the stairs, careful as I feel for each step with the toe of my sneaker. "If we're segregating food items, then I obviously get a cupboard to myself."

He crowds against my back, and despite the energy I just drained off him, little sparks nip against my skin. Is it the storm that's still on its way here? Will he need to be drained again tonight?

I elbow him as best I can with my arms full. “Back off. You’re going to make me trip.”

“Then I’ll catch you.” His hands cup my ribcage, the tip of his fingers brushing my breasts.

My nipples tighten, treacherous succubus body, and I wiggle to get away. Beneath my sneaker, the expected stair disappears. Heart in my throat, I drop the kitchen box, arms flailing for the banister, and my fingers slip across the slick wood. Kellen, true to his word, catches me.

By my boobs.

The pounding of my pulse makes his words muffled as I stare down the last three steps to the second story landing. My box lays on its side, the cardboard flips open to spill out boxes of crackers, spices, and plastic containers of baking goods. Thank god for containers with latch locks or flour and sugar would be all over the place.

Kellen squeezes the plump masses in his hands as he pulls me back against his chest, his breath warm against my ear. “Did you do that on purpose?”

Annoyed, I elbow him harder this time. “Get off!”

“I’d love to.” He bends and scoops me under the knees to carry me princess style down to the landing and turns right. “We can use Emil’s room.”

I shove against his chest. "I meant get your hands off me!"

He stares down at me, his brow furrowed. "Then, how am I supposed to get you naked?" His eyes widen. "Oh, do you want to perform a strip tease as a thank you for the rescue?"

He boosts me higher as he fumbles with Emil's door, and I kick against the wall to dislodge myself. Surprised, he drops me. The hardwood floor slams into my ass, pain shooting up my tailbone.

I glare up at him. "Smooth move, asshole."

His hands go to his hips as he returns my glare. "What did you expect to happen with all that fussing? Is this some kind of role play thing? Do you come with a manual?"

Groaning, I sit up, then scramble to my feet, unwilling to look like one of those stupid romance covers as I grovel at the stud's feet. "It's not role play when I say to get your hands off me."

"Really?" He runs a hand through his dark-red hair, back to confused. "But you're a succubus. Why wouldn't you want sex?"

I lift an incredulous eyebrow. "Because I'm not hungry?"

"Are you speaking a foreign language now?" He

gestures at my body. "You're specifically made to want sex."

My spine snaps straight. "Well excuse me for not living up to your slutty expectations."

His head pulls back in affront at the idea. "Succubi aren't sluts."

"Then why the hell would you just assume—"

A loud growl cuts me off and moist breath blows across the back of my neck. Kellen's eyes shift over my shoulder, and his hands come up. "Don't move."

"What the fuck is behind me?" I hiss. My bones rattle with warning, and my knees lock as something snuffles my head.

"Tac, this is our new housemate." Kellen reaches past me, arms on either side of my head, as he coos. "Please don't eat her."

"Is this another joke?" I demand.

"Nope." Kellen keeps his gaze focused on the thing behind me, his voice gentle. "Tac didn't like the last succubus who lived here, so he mostly stays in Emil's room, now."

"And you thought it was a good idea to come here for sex?" A loud rumble vibrates through me, like a chainsaw on steroids.

Kellen's gaze flicks to me. "I might have been thinking with my dick."

Might have, I mouth back.

One side of his mouth kicks up. "Here, turn around slowly so Tac can get a good snuffle in."

Something large, cold, and damp presses against the back of my neck, followed by a hint of fang that feels longer than my arm. "No, I'm good."

"Don't be a baby." Kellen's knee bumps against my thigh. "Tac's a big marshmallow. Aren't you boy?"

The vibration increases until my entire body shakes with it. Slowly, I inch around. A giant cat blinks emerald eyes the size of my head, and the chainsaw noise, which I now realize was his purr, cuts off.

Lips pull back to reveal fangs that really are as long as my forearm as it leans in close. I freeze in place as moist air that smells like iron washes over my face. It reminds me of the butcher shop, and I suddenly worry I look like lunch.

Black, fur-covered wings rustle, giant hooked tips latching onto the doorframe to block all view of Emil's room.

"Don't worry," I whisper to the beast. "I don't want to invade your domain."

As if in understanding, it blinks again, and its head drops as it sniffs along my throat, dangerously close to my pounding pulse.

My hair flutters with each of its exhales before it drops lower to nose along my chest and stomach, then drops to nudge between my thighs.

"No! Bad kitty!" Instinctively, I push its giant head away from my crotch, and it rears back with a loud huff.

I freeze once more, and Kellen's body stiffens against my back. Then, a loud purr rumbles from the cat's throat, and its massive head presses against my chest, tufted ears flicking.

"Aww, he likes you." Kellen reaches past me to rub between its ears. "What a good kitty. Such a good kitty."

Tentatively, I lift a hand to rub one ear, the fur silky soft beneath my palm. "It's nice to meet you, Tac."

The purr increases, and his head nudges against my chest, making Kellen and me both stumble back a pace.

Kellen catches his balance, hands on my shoulders. "Do you want to come down for lunch, big guy? There's a frozen rump roast with your name on it."

The cat stalks forward, and we press against the wall to let him by. His soft, black fur becomes smothering in the too small hallway, and for a long moment, I can't breathe. Then, he passes, long tail catching on Emil's door and swinging it shut before I can get a peek into the ice demon's bedroom.

I stare after Tac for a moment before going to my upended kitchen box and stuffing the items back inside.

Looks like I have four roommates to contend with now.

Yes/Maybe/No

I keep a wary eye on the giant cat-bat thing as it rumbles happily over a beef roast Kellen pulled out. A quick peek inside shows the entire freezer packed with paper-wrapped butcher packages.

Tac now lays on the wide expanse of tiles in front of the archway that leads back to the family room. It clasps the roast between its front paws as it gnaws on the frozen meat.

I shudder as a glob falls onto the pristine white tiles. "Emil's really okay with that?"

Kellen glances over his shoulder and shrugs. "Tac licks the floor clean when he's done."

"Eww." I make a mental note to always wear shoes in the kitchen.

"And the cleaners bleach the floor when they come." Kellen turns back to the box of pastries open in front of him and makes a happy rumble of his own as he selects a chocolate-filled croissant. He gestures to the cheese danish and a maple bar that still rests inside the grease-stained cardboard. "Sure you don't want one?"

Tearing my greedy gaze away, I unpack my box. "I'm good."

The one he gave me earlier was enough to get me salivating again, but I refuse to acknowledge it lest he decide I still owe him payment for the treat he stuffed into my mouth to quiet me. Though, I'd argue my silence was payment enough.

I pull out the far less appealing box of crackers, the corner dented from its tumble down the stairs. Next comes the dry erase board. Thankfully, the pen still remains attached to the top, and I bring it and my crackers around to the other side of the bar to perch on the stool beside Kellen.

"So, what are the house rules?" I ask as I pull the cap off the pen and poise it over the newly cleaned surface.

Kellen's eyebrows arch up into his hairline. "Rules?"

"Yeah." I roll my wrist. "You know, like shower times, shared items in the fridge, when to feed Tac. Rules."

He shakes his head in bewilderment. "We don't have rules."

Hooking one heel against the stool's leg support, I frown at him. "You have to have rules. That's how being roommates works."

He swivels to face me and takes a large bite of his pastry, chewing and swallowing before he answers. "We've lived together so long we just naturally know what to do."

I blow out a frustrated breath. "What about when you bring in a new succubus? How does the new person know the rules?"

He shrugs again, a fluid roll of muscles that stretches the soft t-shirt until it looks painted on him. "They've always stayed in their room, and we visit when we want energy drains."

My mouth drops open, and I snap it closed with a click of teeth. "You can't be serious."

"If they wanted anything, like new furniture or special foods, they just used the house card to order it." He waves his pastry at me. "You really messed up there in your contract. You could have negotiated a weekly allowance and visits from a massage therapist."

"Not at the price you guys offered." I sniff and lean over my whiteboard to write Tac in neat letters.

"Let's start with the beast. Who's responsible for feeding him?"

"Don't call him that. You'll hurt his feelings." Kellen tosses the pastry back into the box. "He's not some kind of monster, you know."

I turn to stare at the fur-covered wings that rest close to its back and the tufted ears the size of my head. Standing, Tac can look me square in the eye. "You have a winged cat that's the size of a horse. How is it not a monster of some kind?"

"I found him as a kitten. He was only this big." Kellen holds his hands out a shoulder width apart. "The real monster is the one who threw him into the sea to drown."

My chest tightens at the very thought, and my eyes drop. "I'm sorry. You're right. I didn't know."

"I mean, he'd only devoured two knights. But it wasn't his fault." Kellen makes kissy noises at the cat. "They attacked him, he had to defend himself."

"Knights?"

"Yeah, you know." He makes a motion like he brandishes a sword. "Knights."

That would make Tac… Really old. A memory wiggles at the back of my mind from one of Landon's video games. There had been a boss that resembled

Tac. I remember it because he complained about having to 'level crunch' before he could defeat it.

"Okay." I draw the word out. "So, who's responsible for Tac? Does he stay in Emil's room all the time?"

Kellen swivels around to place his elbows on the bar and lean back on them, his hard body forming a lean, sexy line of muscle. "That's what he's been doing, but since he doesn't seem interested in eating you, I think it's safe for him to roam free again."

"And how often does he get fed?"

Kellen shrugs, the unhelpful bastard, and his t-shirt rides up to show a thin line of bronze skin. No happy trail for this demon. Just a smooth line of bitable flesh.

"You hungry, Adie?" Kellen purrs, his body shifting until more skin shows. "I've got an hour before I need to go into work."

The burst of speed I put on in the basement and carrying the dresser up three flights of stairs drained some of the energy I pulled from him. The small, empty hole in my belly begs to be filled.

Shivering, I pull my gaze away to fix on the whiteboard. "No, I'm good."

"You don't sound convincing at all." He swivels,

and light fingers trail sparks down my bare arm. "I bet we can make lightning between us."

The tiny pops of energy sink into my skin, drawn to the larger source of his power already inside me. With a shaky breath, I swat his hand away. "Okay, if you don't have rules, I do."

I wipe Tac off the board and draw two vertical lines down it, then label the columns *Yes, Maybe, No*. In the *No* I write *Entering Adie's Room*.

Kellen leans back with a huff. "You're making that a permanent thing?"

"I'm your roommate, not your slave. I'm allowed to have my personal space." I poise the pen over the board and glance at him. "Do you want me to put no entering your rooms?"

"No, you can come into mine any time you please." He winks. "As long as you're naked."

I puff my cheeks out at him, then write in the *No* column, *No sex with Adie*.

Kellen barks out a laugh. "You can't be serious."

In the *Maybe* I write *Kisses, only if Adie initiates*.

"Now, you're just being mean." Kellen nudges the board with one finger to make my pen slip. "How are you going to drain our energies?"

"That's what the second contract was for," I

mutter as I write in the *Yes* column, *Adie syphons energy through touch.*

He slides off the stool to hover at my side. "What's the fun of living with a succubus with those kinds of restrictions?"

"I warned Emil I was troublesome." I cap the pen, unable to think of any more rules for now. "You guys had every opportunity to find someone else."

"Fucking Tobias and his 'she's the one meant to be with us.'" He throws his hands in the air. "I swear, he's so sure of his catalyst shtick that it blinds him sometimes."

I open the box of crackers as I watch him pace. "He's a pompous asshole, but that roommate contract is good for a year, so you better find someone else to fill your bed in the meantime." Munching on a small handful, I add, "I have cousins if you're really hard up for the whole succubus experience."

Eyes narrowed, his steps turn languid as he saunters toward me. He boxes me in with his body, the sparks from his skin nipping me at every point of contact. I inhale the delicious scent of ozone. It builds a fire beneath my skin, a slow burn between my legs, and I lock my knees together.

My fingers tingle with the urge to clear the dry

erase board, and I dig my nails into my thighs to keep myself still.

His head drops, his mouth close to mine as he purrs. "I like games, little Adie. Let's see who can hold out longer, shall we?" One hand pushes through my hair, tucking it behind my ear. "I have centuries of patience to pull from, and with storm season coming on, we'll be having a lot of skin-on-skin time."

After Kellen struts out of the kitchen to get ready for work, I finish unpacking my kitchen box. A quick investigation of the cupboards reveals most of them are empty. An enormous, gourmet kitchen, completely wasted on a bunch of too-rich-for-their-own-good demons.

I run back upstairs to get the next box and grab my cellphone out from the pile of pillows. For a moment, I find myself searching the stack for my favorite purple sequined one before my shoulders slump. It's stupid to be so attached to a pillow. But it was the first one I bought after I moved out of Landon's house. Before I even owned a bed, I owned that pillow. Even if I buy a replacement, it won't have the same meaning.

The phone vibrates in my hand, and I glance down at the text message.

Landon: What color butterfly do you want for the house warming gift?

Brows furrowed, I swipe the unlock and type out a fast reply.

Adie: What are you talking about?

The reply comes back in an instant. He must be on a break from his video game.

Landon: At your new place. Just got the evite.

What the hell?

Backing out of messaging, I pull up my email. Son of a bitch!

I stab the number into the phone so hard my fingernail bends backward. After five rings, it goes to voicemail.

Impatiently pacing through the chirpy greeting, I wait for the beep. "Julian, you asshole! You better call me back! How dare you use my account to invite the cousins over! You're not welcome here, so keep your vinyl-covered ass off my doorstep!"

The phone pings as I hang up, *Yes* replies pouring in from the cousins. No, no, no. I pull the evite website up to take down the invitation. *Password not accepted.* Frustrated, I back out and type it in again more slowly. *Password not accepted.*

Tipping my head back, I let out a frustrated scream.

Why does my family have to be like this?

The shutters on the window spring up, and Kellen crouches on the window ledge. Large, storm cloud wings spread from his back, lightning flickering in his gaze as he searches the room. "What's wrong?"

"Where did you…" Shocked, I stare at his fine, naked body. Strong, lean muscles flex as he leans farther into the room without coming inside. "What are you doing?"

"I heard you scream."

My eyes dart to the open doorway, the far more acceptable access route, then back at him. "It's nothing, just…"

I trail off, not really in the mood to explain my cousins.

"So you're not in danger?" His shoulders relax, and he slumps against the window frame, his wings slowly dissipating into the air. With them gone, I spot the gray clouds rolling in from the east, dark and rain-heavy with the promise of a storm. He pushes a hand through his tousled red locks. "I thought maybe Tac changed his mind and decided to eat you."

"No, I'm good." I keep my focus on his face to

stop from investigating more interesting parts of his anatomy. "You can go back to your room now."

The corner of his mouth lifts. "Wanna watch to make sure I make it back across the roof safely?"

"Aren't you afraid the neighbors will see you?"

"Does that mean I can come inside?"

As he ventures one foot toward the floor, I point at him. "Out!"

"So mean." He pouts, batting his lashes. "What if I slip?"

As if on cue, droplets of rain patter against the shingled rooftop. I tamp down the instant concern and remind myself he's a storm demon. "You can fly. I'm not worried."

He smiles lazily. "You're a little worried."

"Am not."

"Are too."

My phone pings again, and I glance down at it. Not another one. I glance back at Kellen. "Don't you need to get ready for work?"

"I'm going to wear you down." He hops off the ledge, and the tower wall hides his nakedness from view.

Instantly, the rain plasters his hair to his head, the water caressing over his high cheekbones like a lover.

He shivers, his eyes closing as he lifts his face to the sky.

Real concern brings me to the window before I realize my legs are in motion. "Will you be okay tonight?"

"There's that worry again." He holds his hands out from his sides to embrace the storm.

I lean out the window, the wind catching my hair and whipping it across my face. "Well, I don't exactly want the city to be flooded."

"You're safe for now." Shaking his head he turns to walk back across the roof to his own tower, where his window waits, wide open.

Rain forms rivulets across his shoulders and down his spine, drawing my gaze to a truly amazing ass. He peeks back over his shoulders, entirely too smug as he catches me staring.

In response, I slam the window closed, flicking the useless lock back in place before closing the shutters.

(UN)FRIENDLY

"Yes, thank you, I'll be in tomorrow." Excited, I hang up the phone and meet Tac's disinterested stare. "I got another meeting at K&B Financial. I'm going to get my loan!"

He blinks slowly in response.

"Okay, you're right, I might be getting a little ahead of myself." I wiggle with excitement and gaze around the kitchen. "I have so much to do!"

My proposal from three days ago should still be good. I'll need to make a new cupcake bouquet, and my business suit is a mess.

Crap, I need to dig out the washer and dryer. Will the stains in my blouse even come out?

I run back upstairs, my thighs burning. Living here will definitely keep me in shape.

Back in my bedroom, I dump the office supplies

out of my hamper and load it up with my clothes. I'd quickly discovered the movers paid no attention to what was dirty and what was clean when they packed me up and soiled clothes got mixed in with the ones from my closet.

Since I'm running a load, I might as well make it worthwhile.

By the time I fill the basket, it overflows in a large mountain. I stack my laundry soap and fabric softener on top, then struggle to get it downstairs without tripping on the way.

Tac makes no effort to be helpful, sprawling across the kitchen archway with his belly exposed, massive paws kneading the air. One corner of my unpacked box pokes out from beneath him, squished flat as if he tried to climb inside it and failed.

I guess cats will be cats, no matter their size.

"I'll rub your tummy when I get back up here." I grunt as I circle around him.

His tail whacks against my leg, a fur-covered baseball bat that trips me mid-step.

I glare back at him as I catch my balance. "Unless you don't want your belly rubbed?"

He tilts his head innocently, tufted ears sweeping across the tiled floor. When I fumble the basement door open, he rumbles and rolls to his feet in sudden interest.

Shrugging, I leave it open and cautiously feel my way down the uneven stairs. This place is a death trap waiting to spring. If I stay for more than the year of my current lease, I'll demand this gets fixed. Or I'll negotiate laundry service into my roommate agreement.

The stairs creak as Tac follows behind me, his wings scraping against the walls until we reach the open area. With a whoosh, the cat launches himself over the railing and swoops down ahead of me, disappearing into the disorganized mess below.

I glance around the eclectic mix furniture they have packed into the large room. There's enough here to furnish three houses at least. It could be donated or sold. Instead, it collects dust down here like some kind of weird dragon hoard.

Sighing, I pick my way toward the washer and dryer, half buried against the left wall. Occasionally, I balance my laundry basket off to one side as I move a piece of furniture out of my way.

Despite the mess, it takes less time than I originally thought to reach the ancient machines. Nowhere near as sophisticated as the stackable in my old apartment. It only has a large and small load option and a button to turn it on.

But when I pull the knob out, clear water pours into the metal basket. I dump in soap and cram all my clothes inside. Leaving the basket on top of the dryer for later use, I head back upstairs.

Tac waits at the entry to the kitchen, an expensive-looking lamp clamped between his teeth. The delicate, stained glass shade casts rainbows across the marble countertop as he tilts his head left, then right.

His ears swivel, and I swear he smiles at me.

I shrug at him. "Well, at least it's getting use now."

Washing my hands in the sink, I gaze around the kitchen and excitement fizzes in my blood. My canisters of flour and sugar wait on the counter, the eggs on a dishtowel to warm to room temperature. My precious jar of vanilla beans waits next to them, ready to be made into delicious cake.

I run my fingertips over the oven handles and coo, "Are you as ready for this as I am?"

"Boo." I lower the icing bag as an air bubble in the frosting ruins the last arc of the rose petal. "Tac, treat."

The cat's mouth pops open, giant tongue stained blue. I toss the ruined cupcake into his maw, and his chainsaw purr fills the kitchen. So much better than letting them go to waste.

As soon as I began baking the cupcakes, Tac had shown interest, sprawling around the island to stare into the ovens, nostrils snuffling as he fogged up the glass doors in his investigations.

I managed to shove him out of the kitchen with the lure of a tenderloin I pulled from the freezer. When the cupcakes came out of the oven, though, he'd tried to invade my space once more. Over the course of afternoon, we settled on an agreement.

He gets all the rejects if he stays out of my side of the kitchen.

Eleven perfect cupcakes wait in their cardboard box, and a sense of deja vu settles over me. When the front door jingles and opens, I half expect Julian to come sauntering in.

Instead, Tobias and Emil appear in the archway.

I smile at them, a day of baking filling me with so much happiness that it bubbles over to include my less than pleasant roommates. "Welcome home. How was work?"

"Taxing." Tobias's black gaze sweeps over the flour-powdered counter. "Looks like you're making yourself comfortable."

I bounce on my toes. "I have a big day planned for tomorrow."

"Is that right?" Tobias tugs at his tie to loosen the knot. "I don't know why you're bothering."

His annoyed tone pokes at my happy bubble, and it begins to deflate. What is with this man?

"Why is Tac out of my room?" Emil demands as he stops next to the large cat. His suspicious, cold eyes settle on me. "Did you go nosing around while we were gone?"

Pop! There goes the euphoria. Less than five minutes home and already killing my mood.

I pick up another cupcake and the icing bag. "No, Kellen let him out."

"What's all over his face?" Emil crouches and rubs the cat's cheek.

"Frosting or meat." Concentrating, I pipe on the center base, then build the petals around it. "Probably both."

He stands, his hands held out in front of him as if

he's now afraid to touch his expensive suit. "You gave my carnivorous cat cake?"

"He likes them." Triumphant, I swoop the last, perfect petal into place and deposit the cupcake into the waiting box. "I asked Kellen about his feeding schedule, but he was super not helpful."

Emil's focus moves past me, and he frowns. "What the hell did you do to my fridge?"

Closing the lid of the box, I turn to see what he's talking about. "Oh, that's my rules board. Kellen said you didn't have any, so right now it's only filled with my own."

Emil walks forward on stiff legs. "And why is it attached with Duck Tape?"

"Because the fridge isn't magnetic?" I leave the *duh* unsaid, but I think he gets it anyway because his shoulders pull back. "Why would you buy a non-magnetic fridge, anyway? It's a waste of usable surface space."

"So that people won't clutter it with junk," he grits out.

"What kind of *Rules*?" Tobias crowds into the space between the island and fridge to stare at the short list and snorts. "So, you're seriously sticking to that?"

"I'm making my boundaries clear."

Emil's ice gaze skips over the board, and his lip curls as his focus shifts to me. "I don't have a problem with that."

"You're very unpleasant tonight, as well." I open the fridge, forcing the pair to move out of the way so I can slide the box of cupcakes onto one of the many empty shelves.

Why even own a full size fridge if they only store water and booze inside?

Emil rolls his neck, vertebrae popping. "I'm sorry, I don't do well with change. Can we"—he touches the shiny Duck Tape and rubs his fingers together in distaste—"find a more pleasing way to display this?"

I beam at him. "I'll see what I can do." A chill rolls off his body, raising goose bumps on my arms. "I was about to make myself some hot chocolate. Would you like some?"

"That would be…nice."

As a reward for his attempt at pleasantness, I trail my fingers over the back of his hand, drawing some of that energy off, and the temperature rises.

His gaze flicks to mine in surprise before he clears his throat. "I think I'll go change."

"Do you have a flavor preference?" I call after him.

He pauses at the island, one hand over the mess on the countertop. "Vanilla sounds good."

My happy bubble re-inflates in an instant. I'll win him over in no time.

"You're doing a good job handling him," Tobias whispers as Emil disappears from view.

And my happiness fizzles out once more. I turn to face him. "I'm not trying to handle him. I'm trying to make the best out of our situation. You could make a little more effort. I'm here where you wanted me, so I don't know what your problem is."

"No?" He leans a hand against the fridge, close to the dry erase board. "No ideas? Nothing comes to mind?"

I fold my arms under my breasts. "Are you so hard up that you need to have someone ready to have sex with you when you get home?"

His eyes narrow. "I don't have a problem finding partners."

My arms drop to my sides, and I rise up onto my toes. "Then, what's your problem with me saying no?"

He *tsks* under his breath and turns away. "I don't have the patience to explain things to you."

My head snaps back with indignation. "And I don't have the patience to deal with you crotchety, old assholes hellbent on ruining my life!"

He spins and storms back, grabbing me by the arms. His palms burn against my skin as he leans down. "You really think skimming is the way you're going to survive?" His hands grow hotter, power seeping in to spindle in my belly. "These little sips are nothing, and you're too dense to realize it."

"The skimming works just fine." I yank myself out of his hold. "Landon does it all the time."

"Who's that? You're mentor?"

"That's right. He doesn't like to go into Dreamland, so he does it all the time." I rub the heat from my biceps, cold where I hadn't been before. "Julian showed me how to do the same thing."

"But the difference is that Landon *does* go. He's an incubus, and he goes into Dreamland, and he has sex. Because that's what you're meant to do." Tobias throws his hands up. "Skimming is like drinking water. It fills you up, but it won't sustain you forever."

My hands shake, and I put them behind my back. "You don't know that."

"Don't I?" His nostrils flare as he scents the air. "How many times have you skimmed from us since you've been here? And you still smell weak. What you took from me at the coffee house would have held you off longer, but you couldn't even keep it for forty-eight hours."

My lip trembles, and I bite my cheek to fight back tears. He doesn't know what he's talking about. For all his centuries on earth, he's not a succubus. He's digging holes in the foundation of my dreams.

"This board here?" He taps it, smearing the careful lines I drew. "It's meaningless. Skim all you want, but how long have you seriously gone without sex? One month? Two? How much did you drain from the last human when the hunger got to be too much for you? Did you leave any life behind?"

I clench my fists until my nails dig into my palms. "Stop it."

"That's why you starved yourself right? Guilt?"

"No." I shake my head in denial. "I was working. I got distracted."

"So distracted you forgot to eat?" He towers over me. "So distracted that you hired a demon to come feed you because you knew you'd kill the next human you touched?"

"Shut up."

"You want to know why your stupid rules piss me off? Why your bakery plan is going to fail?" he hisses. "Because every day you don't feed properly is one step closer to you going rogue and revealing our kind to the human populace. And then, you're going to get put down. Living here gives you the chance to avoid that. But first you have to grow up and accept what you are."

My palm stings, and I stare in horror at the red handprint that blossoms on Tobias's cheek.

He doesn't even flinch, his stare steady. "Make all the rules you want, little succubus, you'll be in one of our beds sooner than you think."

Kitty Cave

"How much of that did you hear?" I whisper after Tobias storms out of the kitchen.

Emil steps away from the archway. I have no idea when he came back down, and his expressionless face gives nothing away.

He slides into one of the bar seats. "How's that hot chocolate coming?"

Sniffling, I pull the saucepan out of the drying rack. "Vanilla, you said?"

He studies me for a long moment as I fetch the milk from the fridge and pour it into the saucepan. "Why don't you make one for yourself, in payment for making mine?"

I freeze at the offer, then tip the milk once more, adding enough for two cups. "Sounds fair."

Emil folds his hands on the countertop. "He's not that bad once you get to know him."

"Why do you all keep saying that about each other?" Annoyed, I seal the milk back up and set it on the counter with more force than necessary. "Your claims aren't reassuring at all."

The quiet tick of the gas burner lighting fills the silence between us.

"I heard you were in favor of hunting down your last succubus." I peek at him from beneath my lashes. "Why didn't you go that route?"

"I was outvoted." He sighs heavily and slumps forward on his elbows. "I don't blame them. She was grating on the nerves of everyone in the house."

Stirring the milk, my gaze fixes on the blue flame that curls up around the small pan. "Why didn't you kick her out sooner, then? Find someone else?"

"She was under contract." He drums his fingers on the counter. "It would have been more of a headache to nullify it."

"Surely you left yourselves a loophole?"

"Sometimes Tobias is too thorough."

At the other demon's name, I stiffen. My fingers itch to call Landon or Julian…or any of a number of other cousins. But if what Tobias said was true, about skimming not sustaining me, why haven't any of them warned me? Do they care so little for my survival that they'd just sit back and watch me wither away?

My shoulders hunch. Yes, of course they would. They probably have a betting pool to see how fast I fail. Silly, broken Adie, failure of a succubus, unable to enter Dreamland or survive as a pretend human.

I never should have gone corporeal.

"Don't tell me he broke you already."

I flinch, narrowed gaze shooting to Emil. "Who said I'm broken?"

"You're looking a little"—he waves a hand to encompass my body—"deflated."

"Yeah, well, you guys aren't exactly easy on my self-esteem." I straighten my spine. "When someone tries to stomp all over my dreams, I deserve a moment to wallow."

"Wouldn't your time be better served in making yourself more self-aware?" He points to the stovetop. "The milk is boiling."

Cursing, I pull the pan off the heat and stir it until the bubbles disappear before lifting it to my nose. It doesn't smell burnt, thankfully. I mull over his words while I bring out the mugs and sort through the drawer of hot chocolate offerings until I find two vanilla-chocolate packets.

By the time I have the cocoas ready, I'm annoyed to realize he's right. Tobias might have centuries of experience, but he's not a succubus. And if my family won't help me, then there's a library where I can look up the info I need.

Providing, of course, it's in a language I can read.

I set one mug in front of Emil and drop in a pale-blue bendy straw. "Thank you."

His white eyelashes drop as he studies the offering. "You know, in his own way, you could say Tobias is concerned for your well-being."

"Now, you're pushing it." I lift my own mug and blow on it before taking a scalding hot sip. "He just doesn't want to have to find a new succubus if I die of my own foolishness."

"So, you agree you're being foolish?" He takes a sip, and frost creeps down the straw, the steam vanishing in an instant.

Geez. That must get annoying.

I set my mug down and scoot it in front of him. He glances up in surprise, and I place my hand over his, drawing out a bit more of the cold. It's nothing like the satisfaction I get from drinking it from his lips, and now that I'm focused on it, I can't help but think how these skims feel like small appetizers more than meals.

As my hand pulls away, he stays silent, unwilling to acknowledge the small kindness.

I turn the stovetop back on and move the kettle over the flame. "It's not foolish to have dreams."

"It is when you venture forth uninformed."

"Then, I will endeavor to inform myself." With this Emil, I can almost believe he isn't the stuffy asshole he's shown himself to be.

He glances up, his ice-colored gaze serious. "I hope you apply that to our meeting tomorrow. Cupcake bouquets won't get you that loan. And don't think, just because you're my roommate, that I'll go easy on you. I have no vested interest in seeing you employed. It would be most inconvenient for us."

I stare at him, cold cup of cocoa in my hand. "You just can't help yourself, can you?"

With a sigh, I head for the steps to the west tower, cup of tea cradled in my hands. If Emil was right and Tobias was actually concerned for my welfare, then I needed to apologize to him. He'd obviously been tired when they got home. Even demons need sleep, and I woke them up early this morning. That, combined with the unfamiliar desire to be kind, probably made what he said come out wrong.

I take the stairs slowly, trying to convince myself that apologizing first makes me the better demon, not weak, but my tongue curls inside my mouth with distaste at the very idea of saying I'm sorry.

On the second story landing, I discover the layout is the exact opposite of the east tower, with the bathroom on the left and Tobias's room on the right. His door stands open, the light strains of classical music filtering out.

I pause just outside, curiosity getting the better of me as I glance in. The minimalistic look takes me by surprise. While the forest-green walls and dark, heavy furniture live up to my expectations of opulence, the space feels sparse.

No pictures decorate the room. The dark wooden floors gleam without an area rug to relieve the hard surface, and a clothing rack sits off to one side, with suits neatly hung and sorted by color. Next to it, a low bench of some kind hugs close to the floor, the drawer system probably used as a dresser since I don't spot another option.

The large, king-sized bed takes up the center of the room, resting on a low platform that just barely saves it from lying directly on the floor. No nightstands, no lamps. The bare minimum to still be considered a bedroom.

Tobias sits on the floor with his back to the door, slumped low on the ground with his head propped on the bed. His hair looks mussed, the chestnut-brown strands forming dark waves on the cream-colored comforter.

Gently, I tap on the door to gain his attention. "Tobias, I brought you tea."

He snaps around, his eyes narrowing. "I didn't ask for tea."

"It's chamomile." I lift the cup, the steam wafting in invitation.

Suspicion written all over his face, he shoves something onto the ground and stands to circle around the bed. He changed out of his suit into a pair of sweats and a dark t-shirt. They soften him, making him more approachable.

His dark gaze drops to the mug as I hold it out. "What did you do? Spit in it?"

I lift my eyebrows. "Would that bother you?"

"I've already had your tongue shoved down my throat." He snatches the cup from my hand and takes a sip, as if to prove how much it wouldn't bother him. He glares at me over the rim. "Though,

I guess that won't be happening again anytime soon?"

I fold my arms under my breasts. "It's in the *Maybe* section, which means it's not out of the question."

He lowers the cup, cradling it in his broad hands. "And what do I have to do to get it into the *Yes* column?"

"Stop treating me like I'm something you've paid to use?"

Thick eyebrows wing upward. "Like you treated me the first time we met?"

Biting back a smile, I lean my shoulder against the doorframe. "I seem to remember a certain level of subterfuge on your part."

"I never said I was from HelloHell Delivery." He leans closer, nostrils flaring as he inhales over my pulse point. He moves higher and takes another deep breath at the spot behind my ear. "You still smell hungry."

With him so near, I can't help but drag the taste of ozone across my tongue, revel in the taste of volcanoes that fill my lungs. It creeps in, stroking me from the inside out.

Unwillingly, my head turns toward his neck, his hair soft against my cheek as I breathe him in. I don't like this demon. He's rude and high-handed, and I crave him like the last piece of chocolate in the world. My arms drop to my sides, palms against my thighs to stop myself from grabbing him.

His voice turns into a purr. "Touch was in the *Yes* column."

"Skim—" I lick my lips, the heat of him so close I can practically taste the salt of his sweat. "Skimming was in the *Yes* column."

Damn, when he's not actively being an ass, he's far too tempting for my peace of mind. I should have higher standards than this.

"Tell me about these rules. Maybe I was too hasty in judging them." His mouth ghosts the air above my skin, and I shiver, the almost-touch more solid for its absence. Hot fingers trace against the back of my hand, leaving burning lines in their wake. "Shall we press palm to palm?"

I release a shaky breath. "A pilgrim's kiss?"

Surprise fills his voice. "You read Shakespeare?"

His Adam's apple draws my focus, and I fight the urge to nibble. "I watch movies."

"Sacrilege." His fingers travel up my arm and over my shoulder to slip beneath the strap of my tank top. "You can tell, can't you, that this isn't enough?"

My eyes close as I refuse to answer. How could he

make something that felt satisfying now feel empty? Did his catalyst nature trigger something inside my body? Set in motion some function of my succubus ability that had been dormant, that allowed me to ignore the ache of dissatisfaction skimming brought?

His palm settles against my shoulder blade, fingers stretched toward my spine. The heat of infernos rushes into me, and I whimper as it melts my bones.

Slowly, he pulls away, and I sway after his touch. Fingers trail up my throat, blunt nails scraping against the underside of my chin as he lifts my face to his and takes a step back. "Will you come into my parlor?"

My muddled brain dredges up the answer. "Said the spider to the fly."

"You're continuing to surprise me, Adie." As I watch, his pupils expand to block out the whites of his eyes. "Come rest upon my little bed."

"I know how that poem ends." But I sway forward another step to stay tethered to his touch.

I'm a weak, weak little succubus. Even knowing I'll be devoured, I can't find the will to walk away.

My hungry gaze drops to his broad chest, then lower to his narrow hips. Warmth pools between my thighs as I imagine wrapping my legs around them, of feeling the hard press of him between my legs again.

The farther into his room I walk, the more his scent invades me, wrapping me in a cocoon that blocks out stupid things like pride and self-respect until all I see is the creamy expanse of bed. His scent will be even stronger there, his sheets saturated with power. Does it really matter that I'm giving in to his pompous prediction?

My wings shiver against my spine, restless with agitation. I didn't come up here to fall into bed with him. No matter how inviting his sheets look.

A flash of purple catches my eye, out of place in the masculine bedroom. The corner of a sequined pillow peeks from the opposite side of his bed.

Rage floods through me in an instant, a hotter tide than any volcanic eruption.

Mine. My pillow. He stole it.

I push past him, ignoring the startled expression on his face, and stomp across the comforter. Not even the sting of his energy around my ankles can distract me now as I snatch up my favorite pillow.

Whipping around, I hug it to my chest. "This is mine. You have no claim to it."

"It's in my possession." His eyes narrow, the black contracting as the energy in the room shifts from hot seduction to the rumble of earthquakes. "That's claim enough." His gaze travels over me. "In fact, you're in my room, which makes you claimable as well."

"Don't you even think about it," I growl.

I sidestep, and lazy as could be, he matches me, blocking the path off his bed.

He smirks. "This is fun."

With a burst of speed, I side step the other way, but somehow, he stays in my path.

"Do you know why I like that pillow?" he asks in a conversational tone as we play cat and mouse from one end of the bed to the other.

"Because it's shiny?" Panting, I squeeze my treasure against my chest. I will not leave without it. And I *will* be leaving.

"No." The air in the room turns heavy, landslides teetering on the brink of release. "Because it's the perfect size to prop you up while I take you from behind. I'm going to strip you bare, until all you have is that luscious, milky skin. And then I'm going to—"

I dart forward, slamming the hand that still holds the mug against his chest. Hot tea splashes against his font, and he roars with pain. He flings the mug away, and it crashes to the floor in a spray of ceramic as I dart around him and out the door.

His bellow shakes the tower, a rolling earthquake chasing after me as I run down the stairs.

A surprised Emil glances up from his place on one of the leather couches as I burst into the family room, an angry demon close on my heels. On the floor beside him, Tac leaps to his feet in sudden alertness, his wings rustling.

The beast's emerald eyes meet mine, and I swerve toward him, drop to the floor, and crawl under his belly, pillow still clutched to my chest.

"Adie!" Tobias thunders as he charges into the room.

In answer, Tac crouches, his body a warm, furry mass over me.

"Tobias, please, calm yourself," Emil drawls. "Whatever it is, it's not worth bringing the house down."

His feet appear in front of Tac, and the large cat rumbles a warning. "She threw scalding tea on me!"

Emil sighs with appreciation. "That sounds wonderful."

"You stole my pillow!" I call from the safety of my kitty cave.

"Tac, you don't like succubi." Tobias's feet move to the side, and one of Tac's wings come down to block him. "Why are you protecting her?"

In answer, the giant starts up his chainsaw purr,

rattling my bones and drowning out whatever else Tobias says.

Content, I curl around my pillow, hugging it to my stomach where it fits perfectly, and prepare to wait him out.

Pink, Pink, Everywhere Pink

The next morning, I sleep past the time that my roommates get up to leave for work. Tobias had showed an alarming amount of patience last night, and I'd actually fallen asleep beneath Tac, only to wake up later, cold and alone, on the family room floor. I'd crawled up to bed and burrowed into my pillows, the purple sequined one clutched tight in victory, and had my first full night of rest in days.

Of course, that once more leaves me scrambling to get ready for my meeting with K&B Financial. My shower takes less than three minutes, a new record. Luckily, my presentation materials still wait in my briefcase from my meeting a few days ago. I've practiced my speech so many times I can give it in my sleep if I need to.

I should have just enough time to grab my

cupcake samples from the fridge and drive to the bank. No meter maids to waylay me this time. Having a personal driveway sure does save me the cost of parking on the street.

Leaving my dirty tank top and sweats on the bathroom floor, I wrap up in a towel and run back to the stairs, ignoring the plaintive mewl of Tac as I pass Emil's door.

When I reach my room, I stare blankly at the empty fuchsia dresser before remembering I'd left my clothes in the dryer last night. I'd really gone all out yesterday in my effort to clean, and not a single article of clothing remains behind. Not even my black clubbing dress.

Turning on one heel, I run for the basement.

As I take the wooden steps with more speed than caution, they nip at my bare feet, the threat of slivers real. Definitely not a place to venture barefoot when I'm not in a rush.

I reach the bottom, the cement freezing, and pick my way through the furniture maze. Dust clings to my clean, damp skin by the time I reach the washer and dryer. My empty basket sits on top, waiting for me to unload. I set it on the cement floor, pop the dryer door open, and reach inside to scoop the clothes out.

Pink t-shirts and sweatpants tumble into the basket.

What, the…?

I stare in horror. Did I get a red shirt mixed into my laundry? But I don't own anything red. And these clothes aren't mine. Did one of the guys decide to do a load? I can't imagine any of them in pink, especially not this pale shade of rose.

Glancing around, I search the crowded basement, unwilling to face reality until I exhaust other options. But my own clothes refuse to materialize.

My focus returns to the mystery clothes in my laundry basket. The shirt that lies on top of the pile is ridiculously small, even for my frame. Reluctant, I grab it and shake it out to get a better look. Maybe it won't be as bad as my brain tells me it will be.

Across the chest, giant gold letters spell out a single word.

YES

(un)Professional

Trepidation fills me as I clutch the set of rose pink t-shirt and sweatpants I pulled from the laundry basket. The gold *YES* printed on them winks under the basement's fitful overhead lights.

Turning, I clamber through the junk pile and run up the uneven steps, stubbing my toe halfway up. With a curse, I stumble into the kitchen and rush to the fridge where I fling the door open. Relief makes my legs weak as I spot the white cardboard box exactly where I left it the night before.

Then, a hint of blue frosting on the corner of the lid catches my attention. Fingers shaky, I slip open the box and stare at the empty cupcake holders.

In the next instant, fury washes my vision red, and with a screech of anger, my wings burst from my back. My feet barely touch the ground as I zoom up the tower stairs, bypassing Tobias's room, to fling open the door at the top. "Kellen! I'm going to kill you!"

Silence greets me, and I zip around the empty room in hunt of the red headed demon. When I find myself on my hands and knees, peering beneath his bed, reality slams back into me.

I straighten, wings snapping back into hiding as I glance around the room. He should be home by now and sleeping, which means he's hiding from me. The coward.

His power hangs in the air around me, like thunderclouds that make the air still and humid. But it feels dissipated somehow, old and fading.

The lush gray comforter on his bed lies in a pile near the footboard, his feathered pillows in disarray across the silk sheets. But when I run my fingers across their slick surface, I find them cold. If he slept here today, he left a while ago.

A hand knotted rug, in shades of blue and gray, digs hard little nubs against my knees. Pushing to my feet, my head now clearer, I methodically search his room for my missing clothes.

Like mine, his room lacks a closet. The wooden floor, warm beneath my bare feet, glows with freshly applied polish. He has three dressers, all made from solid, dark wood. The drawers slide out on oiled casters as I dump them out, one-by-one.

A chest in one corner defies my attempt to open it, a brass lock on the outside stubbornly keeping its contents hidden. In another corner, a large bean bag chair rests next to a stereo system, a pair of neon orange headphones abandoned on the floor.

Shoulders sagging with defeat, I peek behind the framed artwork of lightning storms in the futile hope of discovering some secret compartment. Wherever he hid my clothes, they're not in his room.

My mind goes back to the hoard of junk in the basement. For all I know, my clothes are stuffed into a hidden dresser or trunk down there. There's no way I have enough time to search for them before my meeting with K&B Financial.

Twisting around to check the clock on the nightstand, my heart lurches as I see the time.

Shit, I need to leave, or I'll be late.

I rush from the ransacked room, down the stairs, grab the pink outfit from the kitchen where I'd dropped it, and run back up the spiral staircase on the opposite side of the giant fireplace. Back in my room, I nibble on my lip as I take a moment to stare at the pink outfit clutched in one fist. Then, my shoulders square as I march to the stack of boxes against the back wall that I'd labeled *Office Supplies*.

Digging out a black sharpie, I get to work.

From the other side of his massive desk, Emil arches an eyebrow as his cold gaze rakes over me. "Am I supposed to take you seriously right now?"

I force a bright smile and put one hand on my hip. "This is one of many uniform ideas I have."

His eyes linger on my breasts where I used a sharpie to turn the gold *YES* into *Say YES to Boo's Boutique Bakery*.

When I arrived, the receptionist who led me back to Emil's office had given my too small, rose pink outfit a derisive once over and wished me *Good luck* before shutting me inside.

Emil shakes his head. "I would reconsider this one."

My hand drops, and I walk toward the desk. "I'll take that under advisement."

The office is exactly as I remember it with the seating area off to one side and Emil's oversized desk on the other. I eye the wall where a hidden door leads to Tobias's office. Right now, it remains firmly closed, camouflaged among the wood paneling.

Should I take it as a bad sign that K&B's financial adviser isn't here for the meeting?

Unwilling to play Emil's power game again, I grab the back of one of the chairs in front of his desk and drag it closer before I take the seat. When I set my briefcase on his desk, the tight t-shirt rides up in the back, and I tug it down once more.

Directly across from him, I notice the odd tinge of blue to his lips, and my eyes narrow. So, Kellen wasn't the only saboteur in our house. My jaw hurts, and I force myself to unclench my teeth and get down to business.

"I'm here today to request a loan in the amount of fifty-thousand dollars as a start-up for my bakery." I click open the locks and pull out the first of my projection charts to pass to him. "As you can see, bakeries in this area have done well in the past, and there's a rising market for boutique style cafes."

Emil takes the paperwork and flips through the financial charts. "What is your current competition?"

My spine straightens as I pull out the map I prepared. "As shown here, the only competition in the immediate area is a coffee shop, which mainly offers sandwiches and muffins. While it has seating, it's designed with two person tables that don't encourage patrons to linger. Boo's Boutique Bakery will have lounge areas, with dessert towers that customers can order to be brought to their table."

I pull out the sample menu. "Here, you can see the items I plan to provide and the price ranges." Out comes another document. "And here is the baseline cost of ingredients versus the cost of sale to more easily see the company's prospective gain."

Emil is quiet for a long time as he flips through the paperwork. "You put a lot of thought into this."

My wings rustle against my spine in excited pride, but I keep the smile off my face. "I'm passionate about baking. People are happy when they eat dessert, and I want to make people happy. Opening a bakery will allow me to do both."

He sets the paperwork aside, and his wintery gaze meets mine. "And you'll have the added benefit of skimming off those energies to help sustain yourself."

My hands tremble for a moment, and I curl them into fists against my thighs. "Skimming doesn't hurt humans."

He glances back at the paperwork. "It also won't keep you alive."

I bite the insides of my cheeks to keep from snapping. Tobias said something similar, but I refuse to take their word for it. Why would Julian teach me to do it, if it couldn't keep me fed long term? I need to call my cousin. Or better yet, I need to corner his vinyl-covered ass to get some information out of him.

The silence in the office stretches into uncomfortableness. At least on my side. Emil looks like he could casually peruse paperwork indefinitely.

I clear my throat. "So, do I get the loan?"

His attention shifts to me. "Did you bring a sample in today? Of the cupcakes?"

My fists tighten until my fingernails dig into my palms, but I force a smile. "I believe you've had ample samples."

Emil leans back in his chair. "I don't know what you're talking about."

Scooting to the edge of my seat, I grip the desk. "I'm talking about all the cupcakes you ate while I was sleeping."

Again, the eyebrow arches. "Do you have proof?"

Springing to my feet, I point at his face. "Your mouth is still blue!"

Unfazed, he licks his lips with an equally blue tinged tongue. "You should reconsider the dye used in that frosting."

My legs shake with the urge to dive across the

desk and strangle him. "I can't believe you ate them all! You knew I was going to bring them today."

"What does it matter?" He folds his hands in front of him, cool as can be. "They were for me, anyway."

I lean across the desk, eyes narrowed. "Then, why are you asking for more samples?"

His lips purse before he mutters, "I'm hungry."

"That's not my problem." I tap the paperwork in front of him. "So, do I get the loan?"

"Tobias will need to review it, but I have no argument against letting you pursue this venture." He stacks the paperwork together and moves it off to one side before he stands. "Now, let's discuss reimbursement."

My spine snaps straight in surprise. Suspicious, my gaze locks on him as he circles the desk to come around to my side. "I'll make monthly payments once the bakery is up and running."

"Didn't I already tell you?" He stops directly in front of me. "K&B Financial doesn't take monetary reimbursement from demons."

Tilting my chin up, I stare down my nose at him. "And, didn't I already tell you, I wasn't going to be bought? I thought we'd moved past this."

His hand lifts to skim cold fingers over my arm,

raising goosebumps in their wake. “Think outside the box, Adie. Just because you’re a succubus doesn’t mean everything is about sex.”

With a shiver, I fight the strange urge to lean into his chilly embrace. “Your first offer sure made it sound like that’s what you thought.”

He cups my cheeks, thumbs brushing across my cheekbones, and I shiver harder. “Your type of demon has a unique ability to know people’s inner desires. A useful trait to have on hand in business deals.”

Pinpricks of ice seep into my skin, numbing my face, and I mumble, “You want to know people’s kinks?”

When he sighs with exasperation, a small puff of fog forms between us. “I need you to take your mind out of the gutter.”

“But that’s all I get from people.” Restless, my fingers curl into his suit jacket as my focus drops to his blue stained lips.

Will he taste like ice cream? Cold and sweet against my tongue? My belly suddenly aches with an emptiness that yearns to be filled with the weight of avalanches.

The temperature in the room drops as his eyes shift from pale blue to white, and his head drops toward mine. At the last minute, he freezes, his lips hovering over mine.

His gaze clears back to normal. “Sorry, I almost forgot about your rules.”

He straightens, his hands dropping to his sides as he steps away. Warmth floods into the air between us, and I want to kick myself for that stupid board I Duck Taped to the fridge. Hunger gnaws at my stomach, the ache spreading with every foot he puts between us.

My wings rustle, ready to spring free, and fly me to him. I want to wrap my body around his and take what he was about to offer.

Instead, I draw in a shaky breath, and decide to ignore the tension in the room as I take a seat. “Tell me what you want.”

He leans against the desk, just out of arm’s reach, and crosses his ankles. “Most succubi, if they can bring themselves to actually work on it, can see more than just sexual fantasies.”

My mouth pops open at the dig, and he raises his hand to stop my protest. “I’m not saying that you, specifically, are lazy. Your faults seem to come from improper training, not an unwillingness to work, which is why I believe you can learn.”

All desire to mold my body against his flies right

out of my mind. "You really know how to sweet talk, don't you?"

"It's not my strong suit," he acknowledges without any sign of remorse. "Succubi can see desire, they just tend to focus on what calls to their nature, which is sex. I'm going to need you to work past that blind spot and focus on desire as a whole."

Arms folding under my breasts, I bounce my knee in irritation. "I've never heard of this before."

Emil studies me for a long moment, his brows pinching together. "How long have you been corporeal?"

"That's none of your business," I snap.

Age can't be guessed based on power level since some choose to spend longer in the demon realm. And some demons, no matter how long they exist, will never amass the kind of power Emil, Tobias, and Kellen take for granted.

As far as the trio of destruction demons know, I'm just a really incompetent succubus. The self-depredation makes my mood plummet. Their assumptions aren't wrong.

"I planned to try you out today, but your attire" —Emil's gaze takes in my outfit once more—"is less than professional at the moment."

Try me out. Like I was the latest tool is his

financial arsenal. "Assuming I learn this trick of yours, how will it work?"

"I'll call you in as a consultant on clients I need a read on." He buffs his nails against his sleeve before adding, "Payment is based on the information gathered."

This feels too much like a trap. "I think I'd rather pay back my loan in cash."

He peeks at me through his white eyelashes. "That's not an option."

I put my hand on my knee to stop the restless bounce of my leg. "What if I'm busy when you call? Or I don't want to tell you what I find out?"

"You come when I call, or you'll face a fine." His hands grip the edge of the desk, completely relaxed. "Three fines, and your loan will be sent to collections. It's not a place you want to find yourself in."

What kind of collections office would a demon run bank have? Somehow, I don't think it will be a simple reclamation of property.

I shake my head in bewilderment. "How do you make money with this kind of bargaining?"

"The same way all demons do." A cold smile spreads across his face. "We fleece the humans."

A shiver of fear creeps down my spine. Sometimes, I forget that they're destruction demons.

That they've wiped out entire cities and sleep just fine at night.

Is my dream of opening a bakery worth this kind of bargain? What's my other option? Live with them until my roommate contract runs out in a year, then go back to sleeping on Landon's couch? Because there's no way they'll let me stay with them once our agreement terminates. If I'm not beneficial to them, there's no reason for them to let me stay. I'll be kicked out and a new, more complaisant, succubus will take my place.

Irrational anger spikes through me at the idea. Adeline Boo Pond is not interchangeable.

Standing, I take a step to close the distance between us, my body brushing against his as I lean around him for my briefcase. My nipples tighten from the chill that rises off of him, and as I step back, his gaze drops to my breasts. Pink spreads across his high cheekbones, hunger filling his eyes.

"I look forward to signing the paperwork." Confident, I turn and walk toward the door, putting an extra sway in my step to shake the gold *YES* on my ass at him. Beneath it, in sharpie, I'd changed it to read *Say, YES, to one more bite*.

When I near the door, I glance back. Ice creeps

along the oak surface of his desk where he grips it tightly.

I reach for the door knob. "Have a good rest of your day, Emil. I'll see you at home."

His voice comes out with the grate of glaciers. "How many of those outfits do you have?"

"I'd guess one for every day of the week."

He smooths down the front of his jacket in an effort to hide the bulge in his trousers. "I'm going to kill Kellen."

I give him an evil smile. "We can do it together."

Self Educate

I drive my battered, old sedan into the parking lot behind HelloHell Delivery and pull into a spot next to one of the delivery vans. Since there's time left in my day, I figure pinning down my cousin to give me some answer can take precedence. I'm tired of these destruction demons knowing more about my heritage than I do.

Flipping open my briefcase, I fling the car keys inside, then slide out of the driver's side door, clutching the leather case in one hand. It looks ridiculous with the pink sweat pants and a boob destroying, tiny t-shirt, but I don't have pockets. My mind spins with possible revenge plans to take against Kellen. It must be equal in compensation to the theft of my clothes and the embarrassment of being forced to go out in public looking like this.

When I circle the building and come out onto the

main sidewalk, a woman with her two kids gives me a startled glance. She then searches around for the nearest fitness club, as if she needs a reason to explain my attire. When none are immediately visible on the street, she gives me a nervous smile and pulls her children away at a fast walk.

I blame her behavior on the mentality of suburban living. In a big city, I wouldn't stand out so much. Of course, in a big city, opening a boutique bakery would be ridiculously expensive.

As I reach the entryway, a bicycle courier leaves the building, and I wait patiently while he hovers in the doorway to don a neon-yellow racer helmet. It perfectly matches the bike locked to the lamp-post out front. When he finally moves his spandex-covered self out of the way, I head inside the office building.

The lobby splits off into two large businesses on either side, with a bank of mailboxes down the middle and an elevator at the far end. Julian's office is on the fifth floor. Call me lazy, but I head to the back to take the elevator. Not like I need the exercise. I have a perfect ass. Thank you, succubus DNA.

HelloHell Delivery is one of six businesses on the fifth floor, though it takes up the most space. Julian even went out of his way to have a special door made that proudly proclaims the company name. I push past it into a sea of chaos, Julian at its center.

He looks healthier than I expected him to after a run-in with cousin Cassandra. Pink fills his cheeks, giving him a dew flushed, sultry glow. Of course, he had ample time to pop into Dreamland and refill whatever energy the evil succubus stole from him.

He barely spares me a glance as I enter. He holds a clipboard in front of his chest and yells orders to the imps who scurry around him. "I need twelve imps at Peachy Peaches in ten minutes!"

He grabs the collar of a petite woman as she rushes past and scowls down at her. "Not you! Come on, people! We're selling sex here! This is a catering job at a hot, new strip club! If you don't look good in peach-colored vinyl, you're not going!"

A short man rushes up, his arms filled with white t-shirts. "Mr. Poe, I have the rest of the uniforms."

Julian snatches one and shakes it out to reveal a giant peach printed over the bust. From where I stand, it looks like exposed cleavage. "Shirts off, people! Let's see how these jiggle!"

Julian waves me over as imps around the room shrug out of their business suits.

I duck a flying tie as I wind through them. "Julian, I need some info."

"Don't we all, darling?" His gaze rakes over me. "Fitness bunny? Please say you have a tail and ears?"

A shirt hits me in the back of the head, and I grab it off my shoulders, ready to toss it aside. But I have second thoughts and tuck it under my arm instead. Finders keepers. I shake my head at my cousin. "Nope."

"That's too bad." He purses his lips in thought. "I might have a set in the office. You can borrow them if you want."

"I think I'll pass," I say drily.

"Of course, you will." His attention shifts over my shoulder. "No, Philip! Bad imp! Boys wear the white mesh! Did you get those nipples pierced like I told you?"

The name pings in my memory, and I twist around to get a look at the imp. Brown hair flops over his forehead and almost masks his giant brown eyes. With narrow shoulders and delicate frame, he resembles a child.

My lip wrinkles in distaste. Julian thought I'd feed from someone like that? I'm almost thankful I mistook Tobias as my meal delivery.

"I tell you," Julian grumbles, "Imps. They're almost not worth it."

Turning back to him, I arch an eyebrow. "You pay them half what you would a human."

"I said *almost*, darling." His foot taps with impatience. "So, what do you need to know?"

"Skimming. I've heard it won't keep me alive indefinitely?"

His eye twitches. "Who's been filling your pretty little head with stories?"

Relief rushes through me, so fast my knees tremble. "So, it's not true?"

His gaze darts away. "Tabitha, remind me to send you to a boob doctor this weekend. We need to fix that chest."

I can't help but follow his stare to a tanned woman with a D-cup, tipped with dusky rose nipples. "Breast reduction?"

"Bite your tongue!" Julian whacks me on the arm with his clipboard.

"The skimming, Julian." When his gaze skitters away once more, I duck to stay in his line of sight. This close, I see the outer rim of his colored contacts as he glares at me.

He sighs in exasperation. "You have to understand how truly pathetic you were, darling."

I rear back, my wings grating against my spine in instant offense. "What are you saying?"

"I thought you'd get over this whole *humanitarian* thing"—he shudders hard enough to bounce the white curls on his head—"you're obsessed with and go back to draining humans the right way."

"So it's true?" My arms wrap protectively around my stomach. "I'll die if I just keep skimming?"

"I'm honestly surprised you've lasted this long." He smiles brightly and pats my shoulder. "Maybe that means it's not just your ability to enter Dreamland that's broken. Maybe you're storing energy differently from the rest of us."

"So, what?" I can't hide the hurt in my voice, and my eyes sting with his callousness. "You would have just let me die?"

"Oh, don't look at me like that." He glances down at his clipboard, then checks his watch. "Survival instincts kick in before that happens."

My back stiffens. "You'd have me attack a helpless human?"

"Take one of my imps if you're so squeamish." He grabs the nearest one and gives her a shake. The peach stretched across her boobs barely jiggles. "You can have this one. I'll even give you a discount."

I back up a step in distaste. "No, thanks."

"Your loss." He shoves her away then nabs a white

t-shirt and holds it up in front of my chest. "Want to make some extra cash and get your freak on?"

"No."

"See, I try to help, but you just don't want it." He checks his watch again. "It's go time, people!"

He waves his arms at the back door and marches toward it, followed by a tide of imps in white t-shirts and peach, vinyl pants.

I follow after him. "Julian, I have more questions."

"No time, darling!" He holds the door and herds everyone through.

I pause to glance in the direction of his office. Maybe I can find some answers in there? At the very least, I'm sure I'll locate the new password for my evite account. I need to get on the website and dis-invite the cousins from the house warming party Julian invited them to.

As if he reads my mind, Julian's hand encircles my wrist, and he tugs me onto the back landing. "Off you go, Adie dear! You don't have to go home, but you can't stay here!"

The one-way door swings shut with finality, and I have no other option but to follow the mass exodus of imps to the ground floor.

I stomp down the concrete steps. "When do you have time to talk?"

"All booked up for the next few weeks." He glances over his shoulder. "Shouldn't you be asking your mentor this kind of stuff? I've already told you more than I have to."

"Landon is…"

"Lacking." He bangs his hand on the metal railing, and it rings through the stairwell. "Whoever's in front better start running!"

"But, Julian"—I hate the whine in my voice as I stop myself from tugging on his sleeve—"how am I supposed to learn anything?"

"Be proactive." The imps in front of him move into a jog, and we pick up speed.

We reach the ground floor, and the imps pile into the back of one of the delivery vans like a bunch of sardines.

Julian runs to the driver's side. I rush to catch the door before he closes it. "I'm trying here, but I need more to go on."

"Self-educate yourself." He yanks on the handle, and I pull my fingers out of the way before he slams the door shut. He leans out the window as he slides his sunglasses on. "That's why we have a library."

The van stutters to life and I back away. “But I can’t read the books!”

“Then learn to use a dictionary!” With a wave, he screeches out of the parking lot.

Whoever decided to put the portal to the demon clerk’s office at a high school showed a new level of sadistic humor. Nothing like messing with the already fragile minds of the human educators by letting them see a lava demon heading to the equipment shed that sits alongside the football field. As I park near the back of the parking lot, my car blends in with the student vehicles, and I climb out.

The lava demon nods politely at me as I hurry over. The misshapen handle, warped from repeated contact with elemental demons, glows red hot. I use a foot to hold the door open while I wait my turn to enter. Beyond the doorframe, stacks of blue pads give off the unpleasant odor of mildew and teenage sweat. My skin tingles as I walk through the door. Instantly, the equipment shed vanishes, leaving the white marble floor of the entry demon hall.

Black footprints scorch a path to the claims office, and I happily hurry past it, glad my ass won’t be warming one of those hard plastic seats today. I skirt by a trio of sirens, the air around them heavy with salt, and duck under an inquisitive tendril of blue hair that floats toward me.

The hall that leads to the library is empty, the double doors shut against casual passersby. Confident, I dig my wallet out of my briefcase and pull out my library card to swipe it beneath the scanner on the wall.

It crackles for a moment before a voice snaps, "What?"

I lean in close to the speaker. "Adie Pond to see the librarian, please."

A loud grunt comes through. "You again?"

My shoulders hunch as I cringe. "Yes, ma'am."

I step away from the intercom as the door swings open. Out zips the crone on her red scooter. It hums quietly as she circles around me, and the sharp brush of nails skim along my back before she chirps to a stop on my right.

Her head swivels independent from her body as she stares up at me, the deep folds of her eyelids masking her sight. "Well, at least you've showered."

Heat fills my cheeks. "Yes, ma'am."

"Come along, then." She revs the handle bars and

zips back into the library, careening around the doorframe and out of view.

I follow at a slower pace, waiting for the tingles against my skin that mean I passed through the portal.

Unlike my last visit, today's library smells of musky smoke and perfume, underlain with salt and a hint of sweat. My tongue darts across my lips with an instinctive need to taste. Dim, ambient light fills the room, the source invisible. Instead of the vast, never ending pillars of book cases, the library is now filled with chests and baskets that rest next to piles of pillows. Sheer curtains break up the space to form reading nooks, the thin, silky fabric fluttering from a gentle breeze.

My limbs shake with the sudden desire to ensconce myself inside one, to curl around a pillow and allow myself to rest.

A grunt comes from my left, drawing my attention as the crone hefts herself up onto her stool behind the checkout desk. The long length of ancient furniture remains the same as before, the top scratched and dull in places, the edge dinged next to where she parks her scooter.

I walk over as she pulls out her old keyboard and

poises her sharp talons over the keys. "What are you looking for, today?"

My fingers curl around the edge of the desk as I lean forward. "I need to know more about succubi."

"Obviously." She waves a hand to indicate the sultry room. "Be more specific."

"Feeding?" My voice rises at the end, making me sound hesitant. I clear my throat. "I'd like to know more about the different ways to feed."

"Imagination not enough for you?" She chortles to herself and taps at the computer. A moment later, the quiet whir of a printer sounds. She reaches beneath the counter and pulls out a sheet of paper, passing it to me. "This should do it."

I read the single title listed and glare at her. "I've already memorized the Complete Illustrated Kama Sutra."

"Glad to hear it. I was a little concerned about what they were teaching young demons these days." She folds her hands on the desk, her head tilting to one side. "What do you really need to know?"

"I was taught to skim energy through touch, but recently someone told me it won't sustain me. Are there any books on that?"

Her lips curl, revealing a hint of black teeth. "Your mentor should have taught you this in the first twenty years of training." Her body spins back to the keyboard while her head stays facing me. "You should file a complaint so they get black listed from taking on any other new succubi or incubi."

"I'll consider it."

While Landon hasn't been the best mentor, I don't want him to get in trouble, either. If he hadn't collected my ball of energy, I would have simply dissipated with the spring storm that birthed me. I still don't know what motivated him to pick me up. Maybe he thought caring for me would be like his butterfly garden?

The printer whirs again, and she hands me a new sheet of paper, this one with a short list of books on it, in a language I can't read. I remember the odd lines and dots that had filled the pages of the books about Tobias, Kellen, and Emil. I needed more than pictures this time.

Sighing, I glance up at her. "I don't suppose these come in English?"

"I have a translation dictionary I can loan you." The skin around her eyebrows shift, and I get the impression I amuse her. She confirms that when she sweetly adds, "It's in Latin. You speak Latin, right?"

"No." She's mocking me, and there's nothing I can do about it. Landon really did screw me over on this whole training thing. "I don't suppose you have a Latin to English dictionary, too?"

"This is a library." She sniffs with disdain. "Of course, we do."

"Then, I'll take that one, too." I wait for the next print out with the location of both dictionaries, then glance back at her. "How long is the check out window on these?"

"One month, then you can request to check them out again."

Great. I just hope the books come with some sort of index to speed up the learning process. This self-education thing is going to take time. While I might have all of eternity to learn, I only have a roommate contract for a year. And I have a business to start. And Emil's conditions to meet.

Nibbling my lip for a moment, I ask, "I don't suppose there's a reference book for how to read non-sexual desires?"

She cackles, black tongue lolling. "Now, we're getting to the fun stuff. What else do you want to learn?"

I lean my elbows on the counter. "What does the librarian suggest?"

Bargain Dessert

A rush of cool air sweeps through the warm kitchen, followed by the sound of heavy footfalls in the entryway. Emil and Tobias must be home from the bank. The rest of the day passed faster than I expected. Time flies when I have fresh ingredients and a gourmet kitchen to play in.

Tac's head lifts, his ears swiveling as he stares at the archway in expectation. One large paw rests over the stem of his new favorite toy, a Tiffany lamp he purloined from the basement. The dragonfly shade looks worse for wear, the leading between the glass pieces beginning to break down under the giant beast's affection. If Kellen is to be believed, Tac used to eat knights whole, so he should be safe with a smallish lamp.

The scent of sweet, buttery sugar wafts up from the pan on the stove, and I stir it slowly to break down the bubbles. Attached to the side of the pan, the red line on the candy thermometer registers just under the Soft Ball marking. My mouth waters with anticipation of the homemade caramel sauce.

I promised Tac a bowl of ice cream later in order to convince him to stay on the dining room side of the kitchen while I worked. When I set the ingredients on the counter to make stew, I thought I'd have a fight on my hands, especially when I unwrapped the rump roast, but Tac merely stared with hungry fixation until all of the ingredients disappeared into the stock pot before he lay down to nap. The dough for the bread hadn't peaked his interest at all, and it now cools on the counter, its crust golden and crackling.

Tobias loosens his tie as he walks into the kitchen. "I see you found the apron I left for you."

I found it on the kitchen counter when I got home. It had come with a card that read *For your bakery. —T.* Tobias's half-assed attempt at an apology while not being apologetic at all.

"Thank you for the gift." I check the temperature on the caramel before glancing at him. "It's a bit frilly."

The white ruffles that edge the flouncy thing stick out so far I worry they'll catch on fire while I work.

But the thin material of my new pink uniform offers little protection from accidental splashes. Safety before fashion.

Tobias's gaze takes in the meal I made, and his nostrils flare. "Isn't this too much for one person?"

My eyebrows lift. "Who said I'm eating alone?"

Emil comes into the kitchen, nose in the air. "What smells so good?"

"A bribe." I snap off the burner, the blue flame vanishing, and lift the saucepan from the stove, transferring it to the waiting trivet.

Interest fills Tobias's voice as he sets his briefcase on the counter and settles onto a stool. "What kind of negotiation?"

Reaching back, I pull the bow free and lift the apron over my head to set it on the counter, well out of range of the hot stove.

Tobias's eyes widen as he takes in my outfit. "What are you wearing?"

My spine straightens, and I push my boobs out to stretch the tiny t-shirt even tighter across my breasts. Until now, I hadn't been completely sure Tobias wasn't in on this prank. "Kellen decided I needed a wardrobe change."

Emil slips onto a stool. "She wore that to the bank this morning."

"You went out in public like that?" Tobias's gaze rakes over my body, lingering on the thin strip of skin that shows at my stomach. "Why didn't you just buy new clothes?"

Irritation slides through me. "Because I'm close to broke, and I know my clothes are somewhere in this house. They're mine. Kellen wouldn't have thrown them away. He's just hidden them."

"So you plan to bribe him for their return?" Disappointment fills Tobias's voice, as if this is further proof of how inept I am at being a demon.

"No." I circle around the kitchen island and hop up onto the counter next to Emil.

The colder air around him makes goose bumps form all over my body as I use my foot to swivel his stool around until he faces me. His white eyebrows arch in question.

"How was work today?" I lean over the counter to grab the pan of boiling caramel sauce.

His eyes follow the motion. "It was uneventful."

"Really?" I stir the sauce as I nudge his seat. "It seemed like it was going to be…hard, when I left."

Icy fingers curl around my ankle, stilling me. "That's a rather crass innuendo."

I lean closer to purr. "Does stuffy Emil not like that kind of talk?"

Frost creeps up my calf. "I believe you can do better."

"I don't know." I scoop sauce up on the spoon and check the thickness as I let it puddle back into the pan. "People say what you wear affects how you act."

"Are you asking me to buy you new clothes?" His fingers slip up under the leg of my sweats, fingers light behind my knee, and I shiver.

"Not at all." I lift the spoon again, spinning it to spool the caramel into the shallow bowl. Slowly, I place the molten candy against his lips. "Kellen inconvenienced both of us today. I thought you might like to help with a little revenge."

His lips close around the spoon, his lashes fluttering in pleasure as the hot candy slides down his throat. As I pull the spoon back, a bead of caramel solidifies on his lower lip. Would it be crunchy like hard candy? Would it melt on my tongue?

Maybe feeding him like this was a bad idea.

Swallowing, my gaze lifts to find him staring at me through his lashes. "I've never had homemade caramel before."

"Really?" I reach out to swipe the drop from his lip. "You've been missing out."

"This is my bribe, right?" He catches my wrist,

holding my fingers near his mouth. I nod. "That's mine."

Eyes steady on me, his lips close around my fingertip, tongue cold as he licks away the sweetness. My heart skips into a faster pace as I imagine how his tongue would feel on other parts of my body. Cold against my warm skin until I absorbed enough of his power to turn him hot.

Behind me, glass rings against the counter and the smell of savory meat and potatoes fills the air. Tobias's voice knocks me from my fixation. "So is the stew my bribe to help?"

I yank my hand free and shove the spoon at Emil, setting the saucepan back on the trivet before I slide off the counter. "No. The stew's for me and Tac."

He freezes, a spoon over the stockpot, and glares at me. "Why would you give Tac perfectly good stew?"

"Because he likes roast." I hurry around the counter to push Tobias away from my dinner.

Tobias's arms fold over his broad chest. "Then what's my bribe to help? This outfit is inconveniencing me, too. I should be in on the revenge plan."

"You only just saw it," I point out. When I glance up at him, I catch his stare focused on the loaf of bread. Taking the spoon from him, I stir the bubbly stew as I ask casually, "What are you guys ordering for dinner tonight? You usually have something delivered, right?"

Emil pauses with the caramel spoon halfway to his mouth. "We discussed sushi."

"A bit stormy outside for that, isn't it?" Outside the kitchen window, the leafs on the trees rustle in a brisk breeze, the overcast sky casting a gray pall over the backyard. Not as strong as yesterday's summer storm, but gloomy enough to make me crave comfort food. The idea of cold fish and rice makes me chillier than Emil's touch on my leg a moment ago.

"I'd prefer stew." Emil scoops a dollop of caramel into his mouth. It doesn't trail back into the saucepan as fast, the sauce already hardening. He sets the spoon down. "I'll compensate you the same amount as I would pay a restaurant."

"Sounds reasonable." I peek at Tobias, who looks conflicted as he glances from the bread to the stew, then back again.

Abandoning the stew, I pull a knife from the drawer, move the fresh loaf of bread to a cutting board, and slice through the flaky crust to reveal the soft interior. A delicious, yeasty smell fills the room and I slather a thick layer of butter onto the slice. It melts instantly to form golden pools in the deep pockets of the bread.

Finally, his shoulders sag. "I'll compensate you as well. It's easier than ordering out."

My wings rustle against my spine in silent victory, but I keep the smile off my face as I nod in agreement and pass him the slice of bread.

I get the feeling these men aren't used to succubi in the house who are willing to give. Maybe, at some point, not everything will have to be a bargain of some kind. If they get used to me being in the house and even start to like me a little, it will be more difficult for them to evict me at the end of my lease.

I tip my chin up to catch Tobias's attention. "If you want to participate in the revenge, you're welcome to join."

His tone becomes suspicious. "At what cost?"

Baby steps, Adie. I sigh and return my focus to the stew, giving it a vigorous stir. "Labor."

"What kind of labor?" Emil asks as he scrapes more candy out of his saucepan.

I poke Tobias in the side. "Get the bowls, and I'll explain while we eat."

That night, we wait until Kellen stumbles home and goes to bed before we sneak out of the house. The HelloHell Delivery's van we parked down the block waits, already loaded with our supplies. I hadn't even felt guilty when I stole it from Julian's parking lot. He really shouldn't keep the keys in the visor.

When we climb inside, it still holds the scent of strawberry body oil from the strip club. Emil tucks his hands close to his chest as he perches on the edge of his seat, afraid to touch more of the van than he needs to. I don't really blame him. The steering wheel feels slick beneath my hands, the surface shiny under the glow of the street light.

Tobias climbs into the back, wedging himself into an empty spot among the stack of furniture.

The drive to Kellen's club, Fulcrum, goes quickly, the streets empty at three in the morning. Even the late night partiers have made it home by now. I park in the alley, next to a side exit.

Silent, we climb out, and Tobias unlocks the club, propping the door open with a large rock conveniently resting near the wall. Probably not the first time it's been used as a door stop.

The dark hallway leads directly to the management office. It has the same feel as Kellen's bedroom at home, decorated in the colors of a storm.

Even his desk is slate gray with a subtle brush of darker gray overlaid to give it the depth of rain heavy clouds.

I rub my hands together. “This is perfect.”

“Grab the chairs, I’ll take care of the desk,” Tobias directs.

Quickly, Tobias sets a box on the desk and pulls the important documents from the drawers, setting them inside. Then, we pull the furniture out to the hall before grabbing the paint cans from the back of the van, along with rollers and brushes.

Back in the office, Emily pops the top off with a screwdriver, then glances around. “Should we do the ceiling, too?”

“Definitely.”

I tip one can over a tray, ridiculously happy the guy at the paint store had been able to perfectly match the rose color of my outfit. He’d given me a condescending once over when I placed the order, like it wasn’t the first time a pink freak made such a request. Although, with the popularity of door-to-door makeup sales, maybe it was more common than I thought. Did people match paint to lipsticks and blushes? How weird would that be?

With three people, it takes less than an hour to paint the entire office. While we wait for it to dry, we unload the van and put his original office furniture inside for safekeeping. Then we carry in the new furniture, pulled from the basement earlier that night.

The spindly, fuchsia desk teeters in the center of the room, its ridiculous, inward pointed legs precarious on the new, leopard print carpet. That had been a special treat when I found it rolled up in the unclaimed section. Who was the previous succubus and what desires could have formed her that gave her such bad taste?

The wobbly nightstands go against the back wall to replace the sidebar, and Emil arranges the decanter of whiskey and the four high-ball glasses back on top. Zebra striped beanbag chairs go in front of the desk. The only thing we hadn't brought with us from the décor set was the four-poster bed.

As Tobias restocks the desk, he pauses, an appointment book in his hand. Flipping through it, he chuckles. "Oh, this is perfect."

"What?" I walk over, Emil on my heels.

Tobias flips the book around for us to see. "He has a meeting first thing in the morning with a liquor vendor."

I bounce on my toes in excitement. "Good. His embarrassment needs a witness, too."

"Oh, it will be witnessed." Emil pulls a glass paper

weight from his pocket and sets it on the corner of the desk.

Curious, I watch as he fusses with it. "What's that?"

"A camera." He takes his cell phone from his pocket and taps a few buttons. My crotch appears on the screen, and Emil tugs me closer. With me out of the way, the camera shows half of the doorway. He shifts the paperweight until the doorway is centered on the monitor. "We'll be able to see his reaction as soon as he walks in."

I dig my phone out of my bra and pass it to him. "Show me how."

The Bakery

My energy wanes as we sneak back into the house. It was nearly six o'clock in the morning when we traded out the van for my car in HelloHell Delivery's parking lot. Now, the sun turns the sky a deep crimson, the storm clouds from the night before still crouched over the city.

My feet drag as we creep up the porch stairs, and a pervasive itch covers my entire body. I used up precious energy to move the furniture and paint the room quickly, but it will be worth it to see Kellen's face when he goes into work today.

Emil checks his watch as we enter the house. "Just in time to get ready for work."

"I'll see if Kellen brought home any pastries for breakfast," Tobias says as Emil walks straight to the spiral staircase to the left of the fireplace and hurries upstairs. Tobias turns toward the kitchen before he glances back over his shoulder. "Adie, do you want one?"

I wave a limp hand in refusal. "I'm just going to head for bed."

He frowns and turns back, long strides covering the distance between us. "You depleted yourself again, didn't you?"

"I'll be fine." I resist the urge to scratch at my skin. Lotion will help, I just need to get to my room and slather it on.

Tobias sighs heavily. "I told you, it's because you're only skimming. It will only get worse."

"I'm looking into that." The bag of books waits next to my bed, but I don't have the energy tonight to begin my research.

"Come into the kitchen." He grabs my hand and tugs me into motion.

"I'm tired, Tobias." My sneakers squeak against the tiled kitchen floor; the effort to fully lift my feet is past my ability to perform.

"I brought your paperwork home with me." He releases me and flips open his briefcase, pulling out a thick stack of paper to set on the counter. Colorful pieces of paper stick out of the sides. "We've already signed, so take your time reviewing the terms, then sign where I flagged it for signatures. It will transfer automatically to the filing department when you're done."

"Really?" Excitement buzzes through my limbs, but it can't fight back the exhaustion. "I'll take a look when I wake up."

"Now, I know you're in bad shape." He grabs me again and drags me closer as he settles on one of the stools, his legs apart. "You need to feed."

"I can last a little longer." His power pricks at my skin, a soothing balm better than any lotion.

He cups my elbows to pull me into the intoxicating swirl of his power. "Pretend I'm a delivery boy from your cousin's company."

I lick my lips and taste volcanos against my tongue. "But I haven't paid you."

"It's in your contract, right?" His breath caresses my face, bringing with it the scent of charcoal. "I can't hold you accountable."

I shuffle forward a step and feel the burn of his thighs against mine. "You'll try to trick me."

His mouth kicks up on one side. "I don't have time to trick you. I need to leave for work soon."

My lips part to drag more of his scent across my

tongue. Today, he's all heat and fire. He warms my tired body, like a bonfire on a cold day.

When he edges close, my lips tingle, my body humming with the memory of his power inside me and the hard contours of his body against mine.

"You fed me tonight, little succubus." His pupils expand to cover the whites of his eyes. "Let me feed you now."

I whimper, a pitiful mewl that slides from my throat. The pit in my stomach growls to be filled. My arms rise of their own volition to twine around his neck as I fall forward, my hungry mouth sealing over his.

He opens to the first sweep of my tongue, and I delve inside to lap at the energy that waits for me. It burns my taste buds and scorches my lips as it slides into my mouth and down my throat to spindle in my belly, a red-hot ball that explodes through my body.

Invigorating tingles flood my limbs, and I tighten my hold on him, searching deeper for the rumble of earthquakes, the shudder of landslides. His hands push beneath my shirt, the cool air against my bared flesh barely registering as his palms sweep along my spine, over the place where my wings hide.

Groaning with pleasure, my fingers tangle in his hair to tug his head back, opening his mouth wider for better access. Something sparks in my core, then fizzles out. Like flint against steel, a fire tries to ignite in my body, but it lacks the proper fuel to catch and turn into a blaze.

I whimper again, my teeth clicking against his as I try to delve deeper. His tongue pushes against mine in an attempt to take control. With a growl, I fist his silky, dark-chestnut hair to hold him still. His body heat boils against me, and that spark fizzles and dies once more within my core.

Frustrated, I pull away. He watches me, his breath soughing in and out through red, swollen lips. I pace away, my legs buzzing with energy, but irritation clouds my mind.

His voice sounds like landslides as he rumbles, "It's not enough, is it?"

"Shut up." I spin around and storm back to him. Slapping away his reaching hands, I lean past him to snatch the loan paperwork off the kitchen counter. "I'll have this reviewed in a few hours."

"Take your time," he calls as I stomp out of the kitchen. "I'm sure you have a lot to think about."

The creak of my bedroom door opening pulls me from sleep. Confused, I poke my head out of the pillow cave, just in time to hear, "Tac, fetch."

Kellen hovers just outside of my room, and I meet his lightning blue gaze as Tac launches inside, wings spread as he dives toward my bed. Squeaking in panic, I tumble off the other side, the hardwood driving bruises into my knees as I land. My bed shakes, and pillows rain down on top of me.

"Tac, heel!" I shout as I roll away.

The fluffy monster rumbles and thuds onto the floor, giant paws on either side of my body. I freeze as fangs the size of my arm gently close around my leg, and he drags me toward the hall.

"I give, I give!" I grab onto his fur to ease the ache in my hip where it feels like my joint might pop out of its socket.

Tac's wings rustle and settle along his back as we reach the door, and he deposits me at Kellen's feet.

"Good, Tac." Kellen tosses a frozen steak onto the floor. Tac pounces on top of it as Kellen bends down and scoops me up.

The air gushes from my lungs as he throws me over his shoulder. When I manage to catch my breath, I punch him in his perfect ass. "I didn't do it!"

"Liar!" He takes the stairs hard, his shoulder

digging into my stomach with every step. "That's private property you defaced!"

"You can't prove it!" I kick my feet, and his arms clamp over my calves to hold me still. "You stole my clothes!"

"You can't prove it," he mocks back.

We reach the ground floor, and he throws me onto the couch. I land with an *oomph*, then push the hair from my eyes to give him a suspicious stare. "What are you planning to do?"

With a grin, he leans behind the couch and comes back with a shopping bag in one hand. He extends it to me. "Get changed, we're going out."

"Huh?" My mouth gapes open in surprise, and I snap my teeth shut as I reluctantly take the offering. Inside, I find a pair of slacks and a cream t-shirt. When I touch them, the fabric slips through my fingers with the slickness of silk. "What's this for?"

"It was a good prank; you deserve a reward." Kellen ruffles his red hair. "And I don't really want to go shopping for bakery locations with you wearing that horrible pink outfit."

The bag falls from my grasp. "Wait. What?"

He reaches out and pinches my cheek. "You're so cute when you're sleepy and confused."

I slap his hand away from my stinging cheek. "We're going to look at bakery locations?"

"Well, I do own a large portion of the city," he says slowly.

Rose pink sweats and t-shirt fly across the room as I scramble out of them and yank on my new outfit. The material glides across my skin and tickles my nipples in delicious ways.

"I'm ready!" I run for the front door, where my sneakers wait. "Let's go!"

"We need to work on your strip tease," Kellen grumbles as he follows at a slower pace. "That was the most pathetic show I've ever seen."

I ignore him as I lace on my shoes. Scuff marks mar the toes, turning the once white leather gray in places. They're not the best fit for the high-class outfit, but I'm too impatient to go back upstairs to dig out something more suitable.

Running my fingers through my hair, I work out the knots. "Whose car are we taking?"

"Mine, of course." Kellen spins a set of keys on his finger for emphasis. "No way I'm riding in that piece of junk you call a car."

"It gets me where I need to go." His disparagement over my vehicle slides off, unable to find traction in my good mood. Eager, I pull open the front door. The sunshine surprises me, and I throw a hand up to shield my eyes. "What time is it?"

"Three o'clock." His hand on my back moves me onto the porch so he can step out of the house and close the door.

My face feels bare without my sunglasses, but I don't want to go back for them. I'll have to be careful if there are any humans around. Thankfully my eye color falls within the human spectrum, unlike some of my cousins.

A charcoal-gray sports car waits in front of the house, the windows tinted black against prying eyes.

I twist around. "What are you doing home so early?"

"Since I had to cancel my meetings for the day, I figured we could still get some work done." He presses a button on the fob on his keychain, and the car lights flash as the doors unlock. "Go ahead, and get in."

Inside the car, his butter soft, leather seats hug my ass. I've never been in a car this nice outside of Dreamland. I wiggle in appreciation. A girl could get used to this.

Kellen slides behind the steering wheel, and the car rumbles to life. "I've seen the map of where you want to open a shop, and I think I have the perfect place."

I shift until I face him, my knees pressed up against the center console. "Does it have a kitchen?"

"Yep." We pull out of the driveway and onto the street, heading toward the business district of town.

My fingers tap against my legs in excitement. "Are there clubs nearby?"

"Yep." He shifts quickly, and the car leaps forward fast enough to press me back into my seat.

"What did it used to be?"

"A sandwich shop."

"Why did they close?"

"I don't know." Kellen shifts again, speeding up to make it through a yellow light. "Now hush, we'll be there soon."

My stomach twists as Kellen zips around the slower cars on the road, blowing through all the lights, regardless of color. But he handles the steering wheel with finesse, used to driving since cars were invented.

"I'm surprised you don't ride a motorcycle," I say to break the silence.

He glances at me in surprise. "Why would you say that?"

I shrug. "You just seem like you'd like the wind in your hair."

He drums his fingers on the steering wheel. "I have a couple in the garage. But I thought you'd be more comfortable in this."

"It's a horrible car." I keep my face serious, voice nonchalant. "You should probably abandon the rights to it."

He barks out a laugh. "Can you even drive a stick?"

My palms brush over the leather seat in appreciation. "I can learn."

"I'll have to teach you."

"You'd do that?"

"Everyone should know how." Whipping around a purple mini-van, he pulls over to the side of the road and slides into an open spot at the curb. "We're here."

I fling off my seatbelt to scramble out of the car, gaze fixed on the boarded-up shop we parked in front of. A rectangle of discolored paint fills the space over the door where a sign once hung, while sheets of plywood cover the windows on either side of the entrance.

An alley on the right hints at a back parking lot, most likely shared with the optometrist on that side of the business. A Thai restaurant shares the wall on the left, with a check cashing place a little farther down.

Kellen joins me on the sidewalk. "What do you think?"

I step back to see to the end of the block. "Is Fulcrum around here?"

"Around the corner and one block over." Kellen points in the opposite direction. "There's a cab pick-up point at the corner, so you'll get a lot of passersby at night."

Excited, I bounce on my toes. "Can we go inside?"

"Wouldn't be much point if we didn't." Kellen walks to the alley with me close on his heels.

As I suspected, it's wide enough for a car to drive down, and I spot the parking lot at the back. We stop halfway down, next to a side entrance, and Kellen unlocks the door. He pushes it open, then reaches through to flip on a light before gesturing me inside.

We enter directly into the kitchen. The door to a large refrigerator takes up one wall, with a short hallway leading back to an office space. Stainless steel counter tops fill the kitchen, with matching stainless steel appliances on the left wall. A mixer big enough to crawl inside of rests against the refrigerator wall, with a large scale and a wheeled cart beside it.

A pass-through in the wall opens into the front of the shop. When we venture through a swinging door into the main room, Kellen turns on another set of lights to illuminate the space. A cashier's station separates the kitchen from the rest of the room, with a glass display case attached. A chalk menu board hangs on the wall above the pass-through, remnants of the previous owners still drawn out on its black surface.

Booths line the walls, with round tables in the center of the room. It has a fifties feel to it, with red and white stripes and a checkerboard floor. With a little rearranging and some new upholstery, I can easily envision the boutique lounge I want to create.

Hands clasped over my chest, I spin to face Kellen. "It's perfect!"

His gaze travels around the room. "I thought it might be, though there's a couple other places that need a little more work that I can show you."

"No, this is it." My body vibrates with the rightness of it. This will become Boo's Boutique Bakery. If I play my cards right, I can be open by next month. I throw my arms around Kellen's waist. "Thank you!"

"The lease isn't cheap," he warns as his arms fold around me in a prickly, static-filled hug.

I pull back from him to put my hands on my hips. "I know what the location is worth. Don't think you'll hoodwink me."

He points a long finger at me. "And don't think I'll cut you a deal just because I want to have electric, demon sex with you."

"Sounds like we have some negotiating to do." I gesture to one of the tables. "Shall we?"

Demon in the Bakery

It only takes three hours to come to terms on a lease price we both agree on, and Kellen produces the paperwork from out of nowhere for me to sign. After that, the bakery is mine.

The next two weeks pass in a blur of color swatches and meetings with contractors. I spend most days at the bakery, while perfecting my recipes at night. Not even Emil can keep up with all the sweets.

Everything seems to be going fine until I go to check the temperature accuracy on the ovens at the shop and discover one of them won't turn on.

Crouched in front of the oven on the far right of the wall, I fiddle with the temperature setting to see if it will get hotter. If it's just the gauge then that should be an easy fix. But if something's wrong with the elements, I'll have to call a repairman, which means scaling back on some of the nice fixtures I want in order to cover the unexpected cost.

I stick my hand in the oven, frustrated when it stays barely warmer than the room temperature. I've never worked with this model, not that I have any experience with commercial grade ovens. Don't they usually have elements? The avocado enamel on the doors, which I took to be retro chic, might actually be just old.

Standing, I nudge the door closed with my foot and go to the stack of manuals I found stuffed in the desk someone shoved into a corner of the pantry.

Apparently, I'll need to figure out how to configure an office and break room out of the space, too. In my excitement over all the pre-existing amenities, I missed that the shop doesn't have those.

I flip through the manuals in the vain hope I'll find one for the ovens that could at least give me a starting point. They don't even have a brand name on them. Everything has a brand name. And serial numbers. How am I going to know who to call for repairs? I kick myself for not checking the appliances before signing the contract, and for not checking out the other locations Kellen offered to show me.

Please don't let my insta-love of this place be wrong.

The pass-through draws my gaze. It gives me a perfect view of the main room of my new store, and my chest tightens. This can't be a bad decision. It feels too right.

So many items still fill my to-do list, and mentally adding *oven repair* somehow makes it feel insurmountable. The ache in my head, soothed by my arrival in the quiet shop after the contractors packed up for the evening, presses back in.

Overhead, the AC kicks on to blow cold air down on my head. In only a tank top, I shiver at the sudden blast and take it as my cue to leave. Nothing more can be accomplished here tonight. But I can go home and make an action plan. Bullet point my priority list.

I grab my bag and leave the bakery through the side door that exits into a shadow-covered alley, the building next door too close to let the summer sun reach the ground. Despite the shade, heat blasts the chill off my skin, and I sigh with relief. I don't like being cold. It usually means I'm hungry, which puts both me and any nearby humans at risk.

Just to be safe, I pull my sunglasses out of my bag and slide them in place. I haven't accidentally glamoured anyone since moving in with the guys, but better safe than sorry with the discouraged mood I'm in. It would be all too easy to whammy some poor fast-food worker into giving me all the deep fried pies they had on hand.

My mouth waters at the idea of flaky crusts and sweet, strawberry cheesecake.

No, just because I'm a demon doesn't give me the excuse to be an asshole.

Some days, it's harder to convince myself of that, especially with all the other asshole demons around who feel no need to restrain themselves.

I reach the back parking lot and slide into my old sedan, throwing my bag on the passenger seat. Through the windshield, the heat waves that rise from the metal hood become mesmerizing, and I watch them dance until the inferno of my car finally drives me to turn on the ignition.

The steering wheel stings my palms as I pull out of the parking lot and head toward home. I relish the burn, the way it makes my skin tight and forms bright-red lines on my palms that will fade once the car cools down. Corporeal bodies really are the best.

Summer makes me happy. The first year out of Dreamland, the changing temperatures came as a shock, but I quickly embraced all the highs and lows, with summer as my favorite. Give me long days and tank tops, iced tea and sun spots to curl up in for naps.

When I pull up in front of the house, my mood plummets.

With my attention focused on the bakery, I've spent less time here, and the guys haven't been quiet about their grumpiness. I skim their energy just like I agreed to, but one of them—I suspect Tobias—keeps messing with my *Rules* board. As soon as they accept that I'm not willing to jump into bed with them just because I'm a succubus, our lives will become so much easier.

Shoulders squared, I grab my bag and climb out of the car to trudge up the stairs. In the entry, Emil's and Tobias's dress shoes already wait in a neat line under the bench, and I kick off my sneakers before padding into the living room.

Tac perks up from his place on the floor next to Emil's couch, his tail bapping against the hardwood floor. Emil sits with his back to me, wedged in the corner of the couch with his legs spread out in front of him.

Tobias glances up from his chair where he sits with his feet propped up, a laptop on his knees. "Productive day?"

I can't resist the smile that spreads across my face

every time someone asks about my bakery. "The new upholstery on the chairs looks fantastic."

His eyes drop back to his laptop. "That's good."

And down goes my mood again. Gah. If he's not antagonizing me or trying to get me in bed, he's indifferent. Emil, for his part, ignores me completely as he flips through his catalogue. Between the two, they manage to take up the entire living room. My wings rustle against my spine in irritation. I really need to drag my couch down here so I have somewhere to sit, too.

My hands move to my hips. "Where's the phone book?"

Emil pauses mid page turn. "The what?"

"Phone book." I make a large rectangle in the air in front of me. "Large book with numbers in it."

Emil's head turns, and I picture one of his white eyebrows arching with disdain. "You do know what year it is, right?"

My foot taps, and I wish I still had my shoes on to make my annoyance more obvious. "If you don't have one, just say so."

Tobias lets out a loud sigh. "It's in the bottom drawer next to the fridge."

"Thanks." I march into the kitchen and dig it out.

It's much smaller than I remember from the last

time I used one of these, and there are now two versions, the smaller one dedicated exclusively to businesses. I turn to the dining table, change my mind, return to the living room, and stop beside the opposite end of the couch from Emil. Tac's enormous body blocks access, filling the space between the couch and coffee table.

Emil slows his page turns, but keeps his gaze on what I now see is a furniture catalogue. Like they need more furniture with an entire basement stuffed full of castoffs. These guys really need to have a yard sale or something.

Determined, I swing one leg over the arm of the couch and climb over it to wedge myself into the corner.

Emil's icy blue eyes flick up to me. "Comfortable?"

"Super cozy." I wiggle until the cushions cup my back, then yank off one sock and shove my foot under his pant leg. Ice prickles at my toes.

He sets his catalogue down. "What are you doing?"

"Multi-tasking." I shiver as frost creeps up my leg to sink frozen hooks into my flesh and burrow down to freeze my bones. When was the last time I skimmed from him? I count back the days and cringe.

"Sorry for waiting so long. You should let me know when you need your energy syphoned."

His lips tighten with displeasure. "I didn't realize I was allowed to make demands of you."

Confused, I stare at him for a moment before I glance at Tobias, who's black gaze focuses on me as well. Uncertainty fills me. "Of course you can let me know when your energy is too high. That's why I'm here, right?"

The weight of avalanches fills the room as Tobias rumbles, "That rule board of yours is all about what *you* allow. It says nothing about us."

My eyes narrow on him. "That's because you keep trying to sex me up."

"That's because you're an incompe—"

"I've never tried to sex you up," Emil cuts in.

I wait a beat, anger simmering in my belly while I wait for Tobias to complete his sentence. When his mouth stays shut, I turn a smile on Emil. "And look at us now, playing footsie."

"It's been awhile since I *played footsie*, but"—his eyes drop to where my leg disappears inside his pants —"I'm not sure you're doing it right."

"I'll take that into consideration."

With my leg numb from the knee down, it becomes difficult to tell if his temperature is rising or if I'm nearing frostbite. Just to be safe, I pull my foot free, joints crackling as I bend my knee. I pull off my other sock and slide my toes against his bare ankle. Definitely warmer, but snow still prickles at my skin.

Emil sighs with contentment and goes back to his perusal of unnecessary furniture.

Tobias clears his throat. "So what do you need the phone book for?"

"Something's wrong with one of my ovens." I open the book in my hands and flip to the index in search of the appliance repair section.

"Didn't you check them before you leased the place?" Censure fills his voice, and my muscles stiffen.

"No," I grind out as I turn to the right page and find the repair section discouragingly small, most of them listing brand names as their specialty.

Tobias's chair creaks as he shifts position. "What kind are they?"

"No idea, they don't have a label." I turn the page in case I missed more options, but find none. "No serial numbers, either. It's weird."

"Hmm." When I peek at him, I find his attention once more on his laptop.

Well, it was a good effort on his part.

"Are you making dinner tonight?" Emil asks.

I nudge my toes against him. "What do you want to trade for it?"

"Depends on if there's caramel sauce included."

Interested, I dog ear the page and close the book. "Caramel sauce is negotiable depending on what you have to offer."

The next morning, I take my brand-new gift certificate to the local department store and trade it in for a bright-blue pair of clogs with carbon fiber toes. So worth dinner and dessert. My arches sigh with relief at all the new support these puppies give them.

When I arrive at the bakery to meet the installation team for the new display case, shock freezes me in the hallway. Tobias stands in my kitchen, toolbox in hand.

Eyes wide, I demand, "What are you doing here?"

"You said your oven's not working." He sets his toolbox on the floor and carefully rolls up the sleeves of his dress shirt.

I slowly walk into the kitchen. "Um, yeah. I have a repair man coming tomorrow to look at it."

"Cancel the appointment. You don't need it."

"Of course I need it!" I gesture at the bank of

ovens. "I only have five ovens. I need every single one of them to keep production up."

He gives me an exasperated look. "I mean you don't need a human repair man."

"What are you talking about?" I follow close on his heels as he abandons his tool bag to walk to the far left oven and crouch at the corner.

"You either need to replace the whole wall or"—he opens a small hatch on the side and nods—"you need to get a new one of these."

Hand on his shoulder for support, I lean over to see inside. "Is that…"

"Ignis demon," he confirms with a sigh.

He reaches into the hatch and prods the small demon. It lays in the bottom of the oven, a bare flicker of flame permeating its body. At his touch, the demon flops over, tiny arms and legs sprawling.

"This one will be dead soon from starvation." Tobias pokes it again. "Two days tops. The previous owners must not have registered it, otherwise, Kellen would have made sure it was cleared out before he showed you the place."

A hard ball forms in my gut, and my nails dig into his muscles. "It's going to die?"

"It's not really death." He scoops it out of its little home and stands, walking to the sink. "Once it's corporeal body stops working, it will just go back to the demon plane."

"What are you doing?" My voice rises in panic when he turns on the cold water.

He glances back at me with a scowl. "Putting it out of its misery."

"You can't!" I leap across the kitchen, my hands cupping over his to protect the small demon. Cold water splashes across my knuckles, and I use my arm to turn the faucet off. "You can't just send it back!"

His frown deepens. "You can buy a new one. Or better yet, replace the ovens with normal ones."

I bite my lip and pretend tears don't sting my eyes. Something about the small demon pulls at me to protect it, but I don't want to be ridiculed for being soft.

Desperate, I blurt, "I can't afford new ovens."

His brows rise in surprise. "You can't have spent everything already."

"My sigil on the pastry case cost more than expected." Carefully, I scoop the ignis demon from his hands, its tiny body barely hot enough to warm my palms. "I can revive this one."

He turns to lean a hip against the sink, arms folded over his chest. "Do you even know how to take care of an ignis demon of this size?"

Uncertain, I stare down at the creature. "It needs fuel of some kind, right? Wood pellets?"

Tobias straightens, and his hand circles my throat, his voice gravelly. "Wood pellets won't do the trick at this point."

"I..." Lifting my head, I meet his black gaze, and my heart rate spikes. "It needs energy?"

"It needs high emotion." His thumb strokes over my pulse. "We can fight, or we can do something more pleasant."

My tongue darts out to wet my lips. "I need to skim you anyway, right? It's been over a week."

"This isn't a feeding for you, though." His head drops until his mouth hovers over mine. "You can't feed from this. Can you restrain yourself?"

My stomach aches, the ball of energy at my core not nearly enough to satisfy me. I narrow my eyes on him. "I'm not hungry, anyway. Emil was more than enough last night."

"Liar." His nose brushes mine, tempting me with his proximity. "This isn't for you, so your rules don't apply here. Understand?"

I snap my teeth at him. "I'll rip your balls off if you try to pressure me."

The black of his eyes flood outward to cover the whites. "Try it."

His hand tightens on my throat, holding me in place as his heated lips cover mine. The scent of volcanoes fills my nostrils, the rumble of landslides shaking my bones. The power inside him tempts me, just out of reach, and I fight the instinct that screams at me to take control, to shove my way into his mouth and drink him down.

The tiny life in my hands reigns me back, and when Tobias's thumb on my chin nudges my mouth open, I let his tongue slip past my teeth. I shudder as it rubs against mine, tasting of unfathomable power. My stomach muscles clench, heat unfurling in my stomach that has nothing to do with feeding.

His other hand drops to my waist, tugging me closer, and the hard ridge of his cock nudges against my hip, taunting me with the offer of being filled. Blood rushes in my ears, and I melt against him, my cupped hands trapped between our bodies. My breasts ache, nipples hard with the need to be touched.

His head tilts as he delves deeper inside to dominate every part of my mouth, and heat spreads out to my limbs. My lungs burn from lack of oxygen, but air isn't necessary. I only need more of him inside me. I push back against his tongue, and his hand tightens on my throat in warning.

His mouth leaves mine to move across my cheek to my ear. "Settle down."

Teeth tug on my earlobe, and I whimper at the forced restraint.

"Good, girl." His tongue licks up the shell of my ear in reward.

Lust hangs heavy in the air around us. It bites at my skin, little nips of teeth that want to bury themselves in my flesh. My legs shake with the effort to hold back, but what I want is to push him to the floor and feed.

Fire ignites in my palms with a flash of pain.

"Shit!" I shove my shoulder against Tobias, forcing him back so I can turn and open my hands over the countertop.

The little ignis demon tumbles to the counter. It flickers fitfully, bright-red, then dull yellow.

Tobias moves behind me, hands on my hips to pull my ass against his hard cock. It feels good, shockingly good, and I glare over my shoulder at him. "Back off, there's enough energy for the ignis."

He grinds against me. "You haven't even come yet."

"Don't need to." I bump back against him hard enough to make him grunt with pain. "The bathroom is functional if you need it."

A smile twists his lips. "You really are a horrible succubus."

I hiss at him. "I told you I'm not hungry."

He's too much temptation right now. If he keeps touching me like this, I won't be able to stop myself from feeding, and the little ignis needs all the emotion it can get right now. It sparks again, flaring blue for a moment before it fizzles back to red.

His hands move to my rib cage, fingers brushing my breasts. "You know sex isn't just food, right?"

"Yeah, sure." I slap his hands away.

I want more in life than to hop from one bed to the next, glutting on energy while being emotionally dead inside.

The ignis flares again, hot enough to scorch the countertop.

"That's right," I coo at it. "Absorb all that yumminess."

Giving up, Tobias's hands drop away. "I'll go see if there are any pellets left in the pantry."

I keep my back turned to him as he walks away. My bones ache with every step he takes from me, and my wings razor blades against my spine, restless and unsure why I keep resisting.

I really *am* a horrible succubus.

Room with a View

A few days later, I sprinkle pellets into the heat resistant box in my room. Torch, the little ignis demon, flares a happy blue as he gathers them into a pile in the center of his temporary home and settles down to eat.

Tobias had stayed silent when I arrived home with the demon cradled in my arms. Emil peeked once inside the box, and the next morning, a bag of fancy wood pellets was waiting in front of my door.

I'm beginning to think Emil has a soft spot for pets. And I now know Tobias likes to fix things. That tool box he brought to the bakery wasn't just for show. When Kellen came by after work this morning, he convinced me to bring Torch into the hall for a game of lightning verse fire, which the little demon enjoyed if his bright-white flames were anything to go by.

I learn new things about my roommates every day, which is more than I can say for my self-studies. The books I borrowed from the library might as well be doorstops for all the information I can glean from them. The demon language is complex and doesn't translate well into Latin, which then translates even worse into English, leaving me with notebooks filled with unintelligible gibberish.

But I refuse to give up.

However, there are limits to how much my brain can take in one sitting.

Rolling over in my bed, my shoulder butts up against Tac, who's decided my room is his while Emil is out of the house. He doesn't listen to boundaries, though we'd gotten into a serious discussion that involved my slipper and his nose when I caught him munching on one of my pillows.

I stare up in satisfaction at the twinkle lights that wrap around the overhead beams. They give off a soft glow, and when I lay in just the right place on my bed, they form a shining star, the pentagram form now obvious.

Boxes stack on either side of the horrible dresser to give it more stability. At some point, I'll need to anchor the damn thing to the wall to keep it from falling over, but at least my clothes now have a place to go. They had reappeared outside my door the day after I signed for the bakery, with a couple new pieces slipped into the basket.

The couch sits off to one side, close to the doorway. I'm biding my time before I drag it downstairs to the living room, where I already scoped out a nice place for it next to the fireplace.

I really should get back to studying. There's not much else I can do until the flooring people finish at the shop.

But first…

I climb off the bed and grab a box of crackers from my nightstand. The clock beside it reads two in the afternoon. Perfect timing. I walk to the western-facing window and crack open the shutter. Kellen's right, it gives a perfect view into his room.

The red-headed demon strolls in and out of sight as he gets ready to head to the club for the night. His muscles really are magnificent. His golden skin ripples over them, smooth and hairless.

I pop a cracker into my mouth, enjoying the saltiness as Kellen comes back into view, bare ass on full display. Yeah, living here might be tolerable.

The End…For Now.

Continue the series with the next book, Succubus Studies, book 2 in The (un)Lucky Succubus.

Succubus Studies
The (un)Lucky Succubus Book 2

Despite now living with three sexy demons of destruction, and signing the paperwork for her bakery, Succubus Adie can't find peace. The dream of her bakery is within reach, but she also needs to find time to put in some self-study. Too bad for her she can't even read the demon manuals, and no one is willing to help.

With bakery renovations underway, she now needs to find employees who won't look at her funny when they discover the ovens are run by a fire demon, or who question the cupcakes she leaves out as offerings at night. When her cousin Julian calls with an offer too good to be true, Adie has little choice but to accept.

Meanwhile, she's finding an uneasy balance with her sexy demons of destruction, but a summer storm might ruin everything. For the first time, Adie will be called on to do more than just skim energy from her bad boys.

Good thing this little succubus is up for the challenge.

Read Now

ABOUT THE AUTHOR

L.L. Frost lives in the Pacific Northwest and graduated from college with a Bachelor's in English. She is an avid reader of all things paranormal and can frequently be caught curled up in her favorite chair with a nice cup of coffee, a blanket, and her Kindle.

When not reading or writing, she can be found trying to lure the affection of her grumpy cat, who is very good at being just out of reach for snuggle time.

To stay up to date on what L.L. Frost is up to, join her newsletter, visit her website, or follow her on social media!

www.llfrost.com